A Book to Die For

RICHARD HOUSTON

First Printing, April 2014
10 9 8 7 6 5 4 3 2 1

ISBN: 1497329116
ISBN-13: 978-1497329119

This is a work of fiction. Names, characters, places, and incidents
either are the product of the author's imagination or used fictitiously,
and any resemblance to actual persons, living or dead, business
establishments, events, or locales is entirely coincidental.

DEDICATION

This book is for Fred (2000-2013) who was my very best friend and the inspiration for this series. I'll miss you, Freddie.

Also by Richard Houston
A View to Die For

ACKNOWLEDGMENTS

I'd like to thank the following people who made this work possible:

Diana Hockley, author and rat trainer, who proofread my manuscript and made so many great suggestions to make it better. Please visit her home page at http://dianahockley.webs.com.

My beta readers, Mary Miller and Heather Spencer, who were meticulous in their feedback to make the story better. Thank you for going beyond a simple beta read with your invaluable critiques.

Jennifer Givner, for her talent and effort to create my cover. Please visit her and her work at http://www.acapellawebdesign.com.

And finally, to Candace Levy for her wonderful photo Jennifer used on the cover.

Chapter 1

It took hours for him to die; time enough to wish he had never read the book. His death should have been quick and merciful. Unfortunately, few murders go according to plan.

I didn't expect to be involved in another murder after rescuing my sister last year, but Fred and I seemed to be developing an affinity for helping innocent victims. This time the victim was me.

It all started on a beautiful Colorado spring day at my neighbor's annual barbeque in the hills outside Evergreen, Colorado. Fred watched Bonnie pick pieces of hamburger from the artificial coals of her propane grill. His eyes never left the burger. She was struggling with a spatula in one hand and a drink in the other.

"Our great-grandparents lived without it, so why can't we?" I asked while popping the top on a Keystone. I had let it slip that Xcel had cut off my electricity the day before. Seems I forgot to pay the bill, for the third month in a row.

Bonnie threw the burnt chunks of meat to Fred and continued. "They didn't have light bulbs or televisions, let alone computers in their day, Jake. Won't candles get a little expensive, and how are you guys going to keep your beer cold?"

"My cabin gets plenty of daylight and the fridge in my motor home runs on propane, so I'll train Fred to fetch the beer."

"Funny, Jake, but seriously, I can help you until you get back on your feet."

I was beginning to wish I hadn't mentioned my power being shut off. I knew Bonnie didn't have extra money to lend as she was a widow living on her dead husband's Social Security. "You're a sweetheart, Bonnie," I said and poured some beer in a paper plate for Fred before taking a drink for myself. "We're okay. I only let them shut it off because I want to write an article on living off the grid. Those back-to-earth magazines eat that stuff up."

She smiled and drained her glass before getting back to her burgers. "You're such a dreamer, Jake. You remind me so much of my Diane. You would have liked her. She was always lost in space, dreaming about writing the next great American novel."

One of the burgers came apart and fell through the grill. "Where the hell is Lonnie?" she asked. "Charlie paid him to do this for me."

"Lonnie Dean? Why did you hire him?"

"It was Charlie's idea. Lonnie owed him some money and he's letting him work it off."

"Better let me do it, Bon," and reached for her spatula. "He can't get up this early."

"The trick is keeping the flames low to let them cook slowly. You shouldn't turn them over until one side is cooked. I also like to oil the grill too."

"I'm out of cooking oil, but I've got some peanut oil in my deep fryer. Will that do?" She asked.

"No, don't bother. I'll manage," I replied and lowered the flames.

Bonnie seemed relieved and went to the cooler. She opened a beer before retreating to a bench I had made for her a few years back. Fred followed, hoping for another handout. "You need to know that I wasn't offering charity, Jake," she said while Fred rolled over so she could rub his tummy. "Margot wants to hire you."

I closed the lid on the grill. "Your sister wants to hire me? Didn't you tell her I'm not licensed to work in Denver?"

She raised her eyebrows and looked at me. "You don't need a license to edit a book. Do you? And you better leave that open. Jonathan told me the burner valves leak and not to close the lid unless I turn off the gas at the tank."

I did as I was told, and reopened the lid. "A book? Oh, I thought you meant she wanted me to work on her house in Cherry Creek." I bent down to see if I could smell anything. "Doesn't smell like it's leaking," I said.

She giggled and took another sip of her drink. "It's not a handyman job, Silly. She wants you to edit our father's book. Margot said she could pay you a dollar a page and it shouldn't take more than a few days. At least it will get the lights turned back on."

"Your father wrote a book?" I asked, trying not to show my embarrassment at thinking she had offered me a loan.

"Just before he died. Mother tried sending it to some publishers several years ago and they all rejected it. They didn't even read it. They just sent us their form rejections without a single comment on the book."

I flipped the burgers and answered without looking at her. "Did she try an agent? It's tough without one."

Bonnie threw her empty beer can toward a trash barrel next to the barbeque, and missed. "That's what someone else told her too, and suggested she get it cleaned up first. She let Lonnie try, but fired him after several weeks with no progress."

She paused for a moment to watch Fred go after the beer can. "Not that he could have helped anyway. Lonnie only made it through high school because of football. I doubt if he ever read a book in his life."

"What about Margot's son? Have you asked him?"

Bonnie laughed and reached for a couple more beers, offering me one of them. "Jonathan's way too busy losing her money with that roofing company of his."

"Still working on this one, Bon," I said, holding up my can.

Fred returned with the can she had thrown and tried to get Bonnie to take it from him. When she didn't respond, he came over to me and laid it at my feet, daring me to take it. I pretended I wasn't interested then grabbed it when he least expected and threw it toward the trash can. It missed its target the second time. Fred went after it again and stopped midway. He could have been posing for a dog show or calendar instead of listening to something we audibly impaired humans couldn't hear.

"Your guests must be coming," I answered, pointing at Fred. "He's the best alarm system money can buy."

Bonnie tried to set down her beer on the bench but missed. It fell to the ground and rolled out of her reach. She didn't notice. "So will you do it?" she asked.

"Of course, Bon Bon, but not for a dollar a page." I answered while checking on the burgers.

"I'm not sure Margot will pay more, but whatever you want, Jake. I'll pay the difference."

I tried unsuccessfully not to laugh. She looked so sweet trying to offer me money she couldn't afford. "No, Bon. I meant I'd do it for nothing. All I need to do is run your father's file through the grammar checker I use and then I can upload to a POD service and get you as many print copies as you need. Just pay for the copies."

What's that?" She was looking at me like I had just used a four-letter word. "I have no idea what you mean by POD. Damn beer and whiskey must be clogging my brain, but I do know Daddy didn't put it in a file. He hated computers and wrote it on his typewriter."

"Print on demand, Bon. You pay a small fee for each copy you order. Tell you what. Get me the manuscript and I'll see what I can do."

She got up to give me a big hug. "Oh, thank you, thank you, thank you! It means so much to us." The top of her head barely made it to the middle of my chest, allowing me to look down at her thinning gray hair. I began to wonder what I had gotten myself into when Fred began barking at a small caravan coming down Bonnie's drive.

"Looks like they're here," Bonnie said, letting me out of her bear-hug. "Margot said she'd bring Daddy's book with her, so you can get started right away."

The first car in the line was an expensive Land Rover followed by a minivan, an old Ford pickup driven by a kid with red and purple hair, and a Jeep Cherokee. I knew the driver of the Jeep. Lonnie had hired me on several occasions to fix things around his house. He was already out of his Jeep and walking toward the Land Rover before its driver could get out, but not before the passenger. She was a pretty, teenage girl who had to be forty years younger than the driver. She wasted no time rushing over to the old pickup truck, but Lonnie didn't seem to notice. He went straight to the driver and was on him like a fly on a turd.

The driver looked familiar. He also reeked money, and even at this distance I could see his slacks and coat cost more than I made in a month. No doubt, a box of the cigars he was puffing on did too. I flinched when he tossed it after getting out of the Land Rover.

Fred went after the cigar like the good retriever he was bred to be. "Well, ain't that a sight," Bonnie exclaimed. "Are you sure he is not part Dalmatian? He knows more than that bonehead about our fire danger up here."

"Who's the idiot, Bon?"

"Charlie Randolph and the girl is his granddaughter. I call him Chuck because the only hair he has is those few strands on his forehead. He reminds me of Charlie Brown. Daddy worked for him and Chuck's father before that."

Charlie Randolph didn't look anything like he did in his commercials. He was the second generation owner of Randolph Motors, and a good friend of Bonnie's sister. Bonnie had let on once, after a few too many rum and cokes, that she thought Margot and Chuck had a thing when they were younger.

By the time Lonnie and Chuck walked over to us, Fred was back with the cigar. I could see it wasn't lit and never had been; maybe he wasn't such a bonehead after all.

"Keep the mutt away, will you? Don't they have a leash law up here?" Chuck didn't appreciate Fred trying to stick the cigar up his crotch after he had refused to take it in his hands.

"Come here, Boy," I said. Luckily Fred decided to obey me for a change and didn't rub up against Chuck's expensive slacks. "Don't worry. He won't bite," I said, grabbing hold of Fred's collar. Being a Wal-Mart shopper myself, I had no idea if the slacks were Gucci or some other designer brand I could never afford, but I surely didn't want to find out by having to buy him a new pair.

Bonnie wedged herself between Fred and the old grouch. "Chuck, I'd like you to meet Jake. He's the writer I was telling you about the other day."

"You're Jake?" It was Gucci slacks. "Well, that beast should be tied up."

"Glad to meet you, Mister Randolph," I said extending my hand. "Sorry about Fred. He must have thought you wanted to play when you threw your cigar."

Chuck squeezed my hand like he was in an arm-wrestling match. It caught me completely off-guard for a man pushing seventy.

"So you're the guy that's supposed to get Margot's book published." His tone was sarcastic and a bit condescending. Apparently he thought his expensive pants, and his imported leather jacket gave him the right to look down on me, even if he was a foot shorter.

By now the occupants of the minivan had joined us. I recognized Margot instantly. She had the same frail figure and Susan Sarandon eyes as Bonnie. I didn't have a clue who the man and boy were.

"Jake. I'd like you to meet Reverend Johnson and his boy. I see you met Charlie already," Margot said.

"Actually, Carlos is my foster son," he explained, holding out his hand and smiling. "I've heard so much about you, Jake. I understand Margot hired you to edit Ray's book. Now there was a character. I'm sure you'll get to know him well by the time you finish it."

My hand was still hurting from Chuck's greeting, but I accepted his gesture and returned the handshake with some trepidation for he was a big man with big hands.

"It must be a great read the way everyone's talking. Chuck was just asking me about it as well," I replied, grateful he didn't squeeze very hard.

Chuck forced a laugh. "We wouldn't be here if she would let me read the damn thing. Who gives a rat's ass if my grandkids can write better shit? Don't get me wrong, Margot, Ray could do a lot of things, but writing wasn't one of them. Why you won't let me see it before you pay some hack to fix it first is beyond me." I could see he was just getting started. One thing I knew for sure is that a salesman's mouth is like a running toilet — it won't stop until someone jiggles the handle. Lucky for us, that handle was the girl he had come with, who now had her arms around the driver of the truck and was kissing him.

"Marissa!" Chuck yelled. "I need your help over here. Get my tank out of the trunk, will you? This mountain air is killing me." It was my chance to escape and not a minute too soon. My arm was getting tired of holding Fred back who wanted to run over and check out the young boy who had come with Reverend Johnson. Carlos had wandered off and was throwing rocks at an aspen tree. It was too much temptation for a Golden Retriever.

"I better get back to the barbeque," I said to no one in particular, then turned to the others, "You guys can tell me about the book when we eat."

"You're doing the barbeque?" Chuck asked.

"Sorry, Chuck," Lonnie cut in. "I kind of overslept this morning." Then he turned to me. "Show me where everything is, Jake, and I'll finish up for you."

Lonnie went straight to Bonnie's cooler sitting next to the grill and helped himself to a beer. "Long time no see, Jake,"

I picked up the spatula and offered it to him.

"You're doing great, Buddy. Don't let me get in the way," he said while opening his beer.

In a way, I was glad he let me finish; grilling meat on an open flame is one of life's simple pleasures. "How've you been, Lonnie? Isn't Shelia coming?"

He raised his beer can in the direction of the reverend. "Left me last month because of that hypocrite. She found God all of a sudden. I think he's giving her a lot more than religion."

I began flipping burgers while talking to Lonnie with my back turned. "Sorry to hear that, Lon. I know how you feel." I wished I had never brought up the subject. It hit too close to home.

"Yeah, it's been tough since getting laid off. Over a year now, still no job and the house in foreclosure. Guess it was too much for her to watch everything go. Selling the Corvette to Jonathan was the straw that broke the camel's back."

"Jonathan?" I asked, dropping a burger on the ground when I turned too quickly. Good thing Fred had gone off with the pastor's son or he would be eating it. "I thought he was going broke?"

Lonnie finished off his beer and threw the empty can on the ground. "Caught him when he just collected on a big job. He said he's got more work than he can handle since that last hail storm. Even offered me a job tearing off roofs."

I started to say something about the job and thought better. I knew enough about roofing to realize Lonnie would never work that hard. "Well, life goes on." I was tempted to pick up the can and try for two points by tossing it in the trash can, but didn't. "You'll find someone else or at least another muscle car someday."

"Not like that baby. I've had my eye on her since high school. She was a present from my Uncle Mark when he died. He had her since sixty-three and it was just sitting in his barn all these years since he couldn't drive no more," he said and walked over to the cooler. "Maybe

I'll just get a dog like you did. At least Fred didn't leave you when you got laid off."

I looked over at Fred playing fetch. I loved him dearly, but I would give anything to have my family back. "How's the job search going?" I needed to change the subject before I got too depressed.

"What search? All the good jobs went overseas and McDonald's isn't hiring, but I'll be okay and it won't be long before she comes running back with her tail between her legs."

I tried to imagine Shelia with a tail, but let it go without commenting on the picture in my head. "I wish I could help you out, Lon, but I'm sort of in the same situation."

"Thanks, Jake, but I'm not that hard up yet. I still have my unemployment for a few more months and I'm close to making a bundle off that poaching reward," he said before taking another drink of his beer.

"Poaching reward? What are you talking about?"

Lonnie downed the beer and gave me a false laugh. "What stone have you been hiding under? Don't you ever watch the tube?"

I felt like returning his smart-aleck remark by telling him televisions haven't used tubes for years, but considering who I was talking to, I let it go. "Reception up here is bad so we don't watch much TV." I hoped he wouldn't go into why I didn't have a dish.

"Someone's been butchering bears and elk and there's a five hundred dollar reward for information leading to their arrest and conviction."

"I'd hardly call five hundred a bundle," I said, trying to think of a way to get him to go away so I could get back to the barbeque.

"Promise you won't tell anyone if I let you in on a little secret?"

I held up my hand. "Scout's honor."

"You're supposed to use your right hand, Jake."

"Sorry. I'm left handed," I answered, then held up my right hand.

He looked satisfied this time. "I made a deal with the devil. It's worth a hundred times the piddling reward. By this time next week, I'll have more money than Shelia can spend, and maybe buy me a Charger like the General Lee. You know, from the Dukes of Hazard. One with a hemi that can beat the shit out of a Corvette."

I was about to ask him what he meant when Bonnie came over. "Are they done yet, Jake?" she asked, pointing to the barbeque. "The natives are getting restless."

"Damn! Those burgers must be charcoal by now," Lonnie's remarks had made me forget all about them.

Bonnie walked over to the grill to check. "Looks okay to me, Jake, but it's a good thing I came back when I did. A few more minutes and Fred would have hamburger for a week. What were you talking about that could possibly be more important than lunch?"

"Just car talk, Bon. Lonnie sold the Corvette he wanted since high school and is going to buy the General Lee."

She looked at him blankly. I expected her to ask what I was talking about. "You had a Corvette, Lonnie?"

"Hey, guys. I've got to use the men's room," Lonnie said and took off toward the house without answering.

I turned to Bonnie who was watching Lonnie leave. "Once a jerk always a jerk," I said and went over to the grill. I proceeded to put the burgers on a platter, then reached down and turned off the valve at the tank before closing the lid.

"Shall we go dine, M'lady?"

"Go ahead, Jake. I'll be right there after I clean up after you two." She didn't wait for me to object and started picking up Lonnie's beer cans.

"Okay, Boss, guess I better take lunch to the hungry horde before we have another Donner party."

Fred appeared at my side an instant later. His vocabulary might be limited, but 'lunch' is a word he knew well. It was far more appealing than any rock.

Everyone except for Carlos and the kid with punk hair were seated at a picnic table on Bonnie's wraparound deck on the far side of the house and out of sight of the barbeque grill. Margot had her back to me, sitting opposite Chuck and didn't see me coming.

"So Bonnie told me she would ask Jacob if he wouldn't mind having a look at it. I hope I'm not wasting my money. I mean it's not like he ever published anything for real, you know." Then she must have noticed Chuck looking past her with a big grin on his face.

She turned, but couldn't look me in the eyes. "Oh, Jacob. I was just telling everyone how wonderful it is that you have agreed to look at our father's manuscript."

"No problem, Margot. It's the least I can do for Bonnie." I could see just about everyone at the table ready to break out laughing; everyone except Chuck, who sat there with a smug smile.

"Is somebody talking about me?" Bonnie missed her sister's remark when she came up behind me.

"Margot stuck her foot in her mouth," Chuck said and smiled for the first time.

Everyone except Margot started to laugh. Even the reverend did all he could to hide it by covering his mouth with a napkin. Then he lowered his head and began reciting Grace.

He no sooner finished when Carlos and Marissa's boyfriend showed up. I assumed he was her boyfriend by the way they had their lips locked together back at his truck, but then with all his lip piercings and tongue studs, they could have been comparing jewels. The diamond on her tongue had to be half a karat.

The reverend looked over at the boy with a disapproving frown. "You're late, Carlos. What were you doing out there? You could have been stung by a bee."

"Alec was showing me his new pellet gun. He can hit a pine cone a mile away with it."

So this is Alec, I thought. I would have never guessed in a thousand years that he was related to Bonnie and her sister. Bonnie had told me horror stories about her great-nephew's exploits, but never mentioned his affinity for punk.

"I ain't that good a shot, Stupid," he answered. "I said it could shoot a mile. These new models are better than a twenty-two, but ain't that good."

Carlos lowered his eyes, looking despondent. I thought he might cry. "But you said you could take down a deer with it!"

"Can I fix you a plate, Honey," Margot said, looking at Alec. Her tone was soft and gentle. "Your Aunt Bonnie grilled some great burgers. Just the way you like them."

Alec ignored his grandmother and went over to the cooler. No one said a word when he popped the top on a beer. "Christ. Don't you have anything besides this crappy Keystone?"

"Is he allergic to bees too, Reverend?" Bonnie asked, after carefully placing her drink on the table like it contained a dangerous liquid that would explode if shaken. "My Diane would swell up like a balloon from a bee sting."

"Bees, wasps, fire ants and peanuts, I don't dare let him out of my sight without his epipen." Reverend Johnson answered, patting his breast pocket.

Bonnie let her eyes follow the reverend's hand as though being hypnotized. "A what pen?"

"Did you grill any onions, Bonnie?" Margot asked. She looked annoyed that Bonnie had interrupted. "Alec loves grilled onions on his burgers."

"Sorry, Margot, no onions today," I answered for Bonnie when I saw her confused look. The booze and too many people talking at the same time were getting to her. "Just the burgers and what you see on the table."

"It's used to inject a dose of ephedrine," Reverend Johnson said as though Margot and I had never interrupted.

Margot put a couple scoops of potato salad next to the hamburger and handed the plate to Alec. He took one bite out of the burger then spit it out and threw what was left to Fred.

"These are gross, Grandma. Don't we have no hot dogs?"

"Oh, dear. I forgot all about the frankfurters," Bonnie managed without slurring her words. "Would you be a sweetheart, Lonnie and start the barbeque again?"

"Gladly," he replied, looking directly at the reverend. "I could use the fresh air."

I could see Bonnie trying to swallow, so I volunteered to get the hot dogs. "Stay put, Bonnie. I'll get them."

Chuck grabbed my arm when I walked by him. "Can you show me where the bathroom is while you're at it?"

I waited for him to extract himself from the picnic table. He had managed to wedge his heavy frame between the built-in bench-seat and the table and was having difficulty getting out. Once we were in the house, I pointed toward the bathroom and started toward the kitchen.

"Down the hall and to the left, Chuck, and go easy on the toilet paper. The septic systems up here don't digest it very well." It was lame, but I felt the need to say something rude. It was the best I could come up with.

He reached out and grabbed my arm before I could leave him. "Forget about the damn septic system backing up, asshole. That's not why I followed you in here."

Asshole? Who does this guy think he is? I pulled my arm out of his grasp and stared at him. "Did I say something to offend you?" I asked.

"Look. Here's the deal. I know you've been freeloading off Bonnie and this book deal is just a bunch of crap to get more money out of her and Margot. So after you get that stupid book, bring it to me so I can get a real writer to fix it. I'll make it worth your while. What's it worth to leave them alone? A grand?" When I didn't respond right away, he upped the ante. "Okay, how about five thousand?"

It was all I could do not to punch him in his fat little face. I started to tell him off when I heard the explosion.

Then I heard the screaming.

Chapter 2

Everyone left the deck and ran out front when the barbeque exploded. Marissa started screaming hysterically. Lonnie had been blown several feet from what remained of the barbeque grill. It seemed to be in one piece, more or less, but the lid was gone. I could hear the sound of escaping gas. The fire had been blown out in the explosion and the hose from the propane tank whipped back and forth like a hissing snake, violently spitting out a stream of propane.

Reverend Johnson went over to Lonnie, so I started toward the grill when Chuck pushed me aside and ran to his granddaughter. "Oh my god, Baby, are you okay?" His speed amazed me for a man who outweighed me by at least a hundred pounds.

I reached for the valve without thinking and immediately felt the pain. "Damn it!" I yelled, pulling my hand away. It was like grabbing a micro-waved cup of coffee; not hot enough to burn the skin, but too hot to hold. Everyone had momentarily forgotten about Lonnie to watch me fight the propane snake — until he started to moan.

"Oh, Papa, I thought he had lost his...," Marissa sobbed.

I took off my shirt and used it for a makeshift glove to shut off the tank, and then checked over the rest of the group before going to help the reverend. It looked like a movie that had been put on pause. Bonnie, Margot, and the reverend's foster-son stood frozen in place, staring at Lonnie with their mouths open. I had to fight the thought of a bug flying into one of them before I realized Alec and Fred were missing. "Where's Fred?" I asked while putting my shirt back on.

"Somebody better call 911," the reverend said, ignoring my question. "We need to get this poor man to the hospital."

Margot reached into her pants pocket, took her phone and punched in three numbers.

"Has anyone seen Fred?" I asked again, this time with fear in my voice.

"Alec was bored and took him for a walk," Margot answered while punching her keypad. "That mutt will follow anyone who feeds him."

I assumed she was referring to Alec's uneaten hamburger. This lady must have gone to the same charm-school class as Chuck. Still, I felt a sense of relief at not having to choose between Lonnie and my dog and went over to help the reverend. Bonnie wasted no time joining us. Lonnie looked like a surfer with a bad case of sunburn. His hair was singed to the scalp. I had no sooner bent down to check on Lonnie when I saw Fred running toward me, with Alec a good fifty yards behind.

"You're not looking too good, Lon. How are you feeling?" I asked just as Fred arrived and nearly knocked me over. His tail was wagging back and forth faster than the pendulum on an over-wound cuckoo clock. He acted like he hadn't seen me in years and tried to lick me in the face. I grabbed his collar before he spotted Lonnie's burns and tried to administer first-aid with his tongue.

"Damn, Jake. Why didn't you warn me about that death trap? Shit, this hurts."

"What the hell was that noise?" Alec asked, grasping for breath. "It sounded like a bomb went off." Then he saw Lonnie. "Holy crap! That must really smart. What happened to him?"

"The barbeque blew up," Bonnie answered. "I've got some Bactine in the medicine cabinet. I'll be right back"

Fred seemed to lose interest in Lonnie and wanted to follow Bonnie. He didn't get far once I let him go. He must have heard the siren. I couldn't hear it yet, but I could see a dust cloud down toward Bear Creek; it was a sure sign someone was driving too fast up our dirt road.

"Please, God. Hurry. I'm dying here," Lonnie cried to no one in particular. I suppose he was talking to God.

I found myself silently praying too when I saw Chuck waddling toward us. He no longer had the speed of a track star when he had pushed me aside earlier. I knew his type: aggressive and arrogant. He would want to dominate the situation and more than likely start telling everybody what to do. I prayed the ambulance would get here before he did. Then everyone became quiet as we watched the dust cloud get closer, and the siren getting louder. "What the hell." he said when a sheriff's truck pulled up. "We call for an ambulance and the stupid idiots send us a county Mountie?"

The deputy was already out of his truck and gave Chuck a disdainful look. "What's going on here?" Before anyone could answer, his radio started squawking and he removed a microphone from his shoulder strap. I couldn't understand what he and the dispatcher were saying. He might as well have been a world-war two code talker.

"I need help! Please somebody!" Lonnie screamed and began shaking.

Chuck spoke first. "Where's the friggin ambulance for Christ sake? Sorry, Reverend," he said with a glance in the pastor's direction.

"It's on the way. I was patrolling Upper Bear when I got the call, but they have to come from Bergen Park," the deputy answered.

"My God. What happened to him?" he asked, staring in horror at Lonnie's face.

"It hurts so bad. Please dear God, do something." Lonnie didn't hold back the tears this time.

He was sobbing like a child when Bonnie came back with the Bactine. She nudged me aside and began spraying Lonnie's arms.

"Don't do that, Ma'am," the deputy said, reaching over to grab her arm. "Better let the paramedics handle this."

"Oh, dear," Bonnie said. "I wasn't thinking."

"Well, no sense in wasting it," Reverend Johnson said, "Hold out your arm, Carlos, so Bonnie can spray that rash you have."

Bonnie pulled back like Carlos had the plague. "Uh, maybe the deputy's right. You better let him see a doctor with that rash." She turned, and went back to the house before anyone could protest. The deputy's intercom started squawking before anyone could stop her.

"Hold on, Buddy," the deputy said to Lonnie. "They're almost here."

"I see you still haven't bought a leash for that dog." The deputy said after the paramedics had driven away with Lonnie. He had taken me aside to "ask a few questions" and Fred had followed at my heels.

His remark startled me until I saw him smile. Then I recognized him, and realized he was kidding. "He eats them faster than I can buy them. I'm sorry, I forgot your name?"

"Hampton. Terry Hampton. We met last year when you had a little problem with someone trying to kill you."

He was the same officer who came to check out my motor home last fall when it had been ransacked. I told him I thought it was the killer of my sister's husband who followed me from Missouri. All Deputy Hampton said was not to let Fred run loose.

"I never did thank you for saving my life, Officer. Lucky for me and Fred you followed up on my story."

The killer had come back and was ready to shoot me with my own shotgun. In the process of trying to hide under my glass-top coffee-table, Fred threw the killer off balance making his shot go through the ceiling. Hampton shot the killer in the leg as he tried to flee my cabin.

"I hear you were in charge of the barbeque." His tone suggested that it was all business again. We had walked over to the barbeque grill, which I thought was amusing considering I was the one being grilled now.

"I guess you could say that, Officer. Bonnie was a little under the weather, so I took over when I arrived."

"And you didn't smell it leaking?"

"No, not really. Only thing I could smell was burnt hamburger," I answered and unconsciously reached down to grab Fred's collar.

Hampton made a few notes in his pad, and then began checking out the barbeque. Chuck had managed to slink within earshot and was listening to everything.

The severed hose on the propane tank was no longer imitating a hissing cobra. It had become a zombie instead. I was sure I killed it when I shut it off, but I could still hear the sound of gas spurting from it every so often. That didn't stop the deputy from walking over to it anyway.

"Don't touch it," I said. He was reaching for the valve. "I nearly burned myself trying to shut it off. It's almost empty, so unless you have some gloves, I suggest you let it be."

Hampton's hand stopped inches from the valve. "Thanks for the warning. Your friend's lucky that the tank didn't explode. I wonder what made him light it."

It was a statement more than a question, but I answered anyway. "Ms Jones asked him to restart it so we could cook some hot dogs. I had no idea it was leaking. I swear I shut off the valve earlier."

"Surely he could smell the gas?"

I let Fred go before walking over to the grill. "Did you notice the smell?" I asked, while pointing to the tank.

"No. Not really."

Fred had lost interest in our conversation when a squirrel in a nearby tree began making chattering sounds at him. He left me and pretended to sneak up on Chatter the tree-rat. Chatter was the name Bonnie had given the neighborhood squirrel who liked to chatter away at Fred from the safety of a low-lying branch.

"Neither did I or I would have never let Lonnie relight it. I just realized there wasn't any smell."

Hampton bent down to examine the tank and wiggled his nose. "And you closed the lid before he relit it?"

"Yeah, like I said I thought we were finished with it, and shut off the gas before closing the lid. Bonnie told me the burner valves were leaking and to turn off the valve at the tank, so that's what I did."

"You didn't turn off the burners?"

"All the more reason this doesn't make any sense," I answered, "Any gas in the line should have bled off long before he relit it. I'm beginning to think the main valve must be bad too."

"What a bunch of bullshit," Chuck seemed to forget it was me who was being questioned. "Any idiot can see the asshole is trying to make excuses for his stupidity. Probably afraid the guy who got burned is going to sue him and now he's trying to blame it on a defective tank."

We both turned and looked at Chuck. My urge to punch him returned, but I held back. The officer might not take kindly of me beating on a handicapped senior a foot shorter and twenty years older.

"You're that car dealer, Charlie Randolph. Aren't you?" The deputy responded, once again holding out his hand.

Chuck's mood changed instantly; his antagonism replaced by a phony car-salesman smile. "Call me Chuck, Officer," he answered, returning the handshake. A business card appeared out of nowhere. "We give all our men in blue an extra ten percent off. Just show your badge and my boys will take care of you."

Under most circumstances, I would have waited to speak. My parents raised me not to interrupt a conversation. It was rude, they said, but I felt like being rude. "Excuse me, Officer. I think I'm needed in the house. Can I go now?"

Chuck glared at me when I cut him off. Officer Hampton didn't seem to notice.

"Sure, Mister Martin. I was just leaving anyway. I'll call you if I have any more questions." He turned back to Chuck. "It's been nice meeting you, Mister Randolph. I'll come by next time I need a car." He didn't give Chuck a chance to finish and left him standing alone by the grill. I couldn't help but smile. I called out for Fred and went to find my hostess so I too could say goodbye and leave.

Fred was by my side in an instant, but we didn't get far before running into the reverend and Carlos. He had the boy by the shoulder, leading him toward the van. I couldn't help but notice the boy seemed upset and the reverend wasn't smiling either.

"You guys leaving so soon?" I asked.

"It's been a long day, Jake. Two services this morning and Carlos needs to get ready for school tomorrow."

"I don't wanna leave, Reverend Johnson. Please can't we stay longer? Alec said he'd take me for a hike up the mountain and let me shoot his new pellet gun. Please?"

"Speaking of Alec, have you seen him Jake? Margot asked me to check on him."

"He was headed up the side of the mountain with Marissa the last time I saw him," I said a little too loud, so Chuck could hear. He was over by the barbeque, sniffing the air like a police dog.

"I'll go find them. Maybe they went to shoot the gun," Carlos said. Reverend Johnson grabbed him by the collar just as he began to take off after Alec.

"Hold on there, Hoss. Something tells me they didn't go up there to do any target practice."

"You didn't stop them?" It was Chuck. He had traversed the twenty yards from the grill to where we were standing in seconds. It looked like he was going to have a stroke.

I reached for Fred's collar when he started growling as Chuck got too close. It was more for his safety than Chuck's. I knew Fred wouldn't bite, but I wasn't too sure about Chuck. His kind thought nothing of kicking a dog and calling it self-defense.

"Sorry. I was a little busy at the time to babysit for you," I answered, trying not to laugh at the thought of Alec and Marissa making out behind some big rock with her grandfather so close.

He ignored me and turned to the reverend. "Let him go, Johnson. I'm sure they won't do anything if he tags along."

The reverend seemed hesitant before answering. "Okay, Carlos, but I'm going too. They have wild animals up here. I can't just let you go running off by yourself. What if you get stung by a bee?"

"Ain't that why you carry the epy pen, Johnson?" Chuck asked.

I had nothing more to say to either of them and went back to my original task of seeking out my hostess. I found Bonnie in the kitchen with Margot chatting away with their backs to me as they washed dishes.

"You two need any help with those?" I asked.

It wasn't difficult to tell them apart. They both stood around five-two and had the same slim, bordering on frail, build. Unlike her twin, Margot kept her hair looking twenty years younger with a little help from Clairol. I guessed they were probably in their mid to late sixties only because of things Bonnie had told me over the years. No one would have known their age by looking at them. They still had the bright eyes and actions of younger women.

"We wouldn't need any help, if she didn't drink so much," Margot answered without looking my way. She was busy stacking the dishes in the washer as quickly as Bonnie could pre-wash them, which wasn't very quick at all. Fred could have done it faster and saved them the time of scraping all the leftovers into the garbage.

"Jake, Sweetheart, Reverend Johnson needs to leave. Would you mind getting Margot's bags from his minivan? She's staying with me for a few days," Bonnie said while pouring the last of her bourbon from the bottle she had been carrying around all day. She didn't bother to dilute it this time with cola like she usually does.

Margot closed the dishwasher door and looked contemptuously at her sister before turning to me. "And the manuscripts, Jake. They're in the back in white boxes."

"Manuscripts? How many books did Ray write?" I asked.

Bonnie answered for her sister. "Just one, Silly. One of them is a copy."

I smiled. I've heard about twins answering for one another, but never experienced it before. "No problem, but it may be a while before your pastor leaves. He just went up the hill with Carlos to find Alec and Marissa."

Margot slammed a dish on the counter, breaking it into a hundred pieces. "Oh, shit. I hope Chuck didn't see them," she said without a second glance at the mess she just made, and ran out the door before I could tell her he already knew.

Bonnie stopped washing and went over to clean up her sister's mess. Then, acting as though nothing had happened, she reached for an overhead cabinet. "Do you mind, Jake? There's another bottle up there I can't get without my step-stool."

I retrieved her bourbon and opened it for her, trying not to laugh. "I better get that manuscript before Chuck does," I said, heading for the door while wondering if Margot knew about Bonnie's stash. Stash was putting it kindly; she had a whole case of Jack Daniels Black Label up there.

All hell was breaking loose when I got outside. Margot and Chuck were arguing. I could hear her defending her grandson while Chuck was tearing him down. I made sure Chuck saw me grin as I walked past him.

I retrieved Margot's bags from the back of the van then found the two white boxes in the back seat, and headed back. I wanted to ask Margot, which one was the copy, but Chuck was still at it when I reached them, so I went on to the house with her bags.

Bonnie was on her porch watching and listening. I set the bags down before taking them in the house so I could watch too. "What an arrogant bastard!"

"He's not so bad once you get to know him, Jake. He's only watching out for us," she answered without taking her eyes off Chuck.

"Yeah. Sweet like Freddie Krueger. What's he got against me anyway? There's got to be more to it." I turned my back to the action and gave her my dumb look before picking up the bags again. It was a habit I'd developed with my ex-wife when I said something stupid.

"To what?" Margot asked before I managed to get back inside. She had given up arguing when she saw the reverend's entourage coming down the driveway with Alec and Marissa trailing behind. Chuck was waving his arms and shouting words a pastor should never hear.

"Jake doesn't think Chuck likes him," Bonnie answered her sister while slipping past me to go into the house. I held the door open for Margot too, and she followed without saying a word.

Bonnie was already sitting at the table with a drink. Margot went over to a kitchen cabinet and brought out some cut-crystal glasses and put them on the table next to the new bottle of booze. I thought Bonnie would have a fit when her sister didn't use a coaster. The table was an old piece she had bought at a garage sale last year. I knew it well since she had me refinish it even though I warned her it might be an antique.

"Care to help me fall off the wagon, Jake?"

I placed some napkins under the glasses before answering. I had worked too hard on the table to see it ruined now. "No thanks, Margot. I never drink anything stronger than beer, and I've had my quota of that."

"Here's to all the grandmothers going gray because of their grandchildren," she said and poured herself a drink and another for me before continuing, "You're going to need this."

Alec came barging into the house before Margot could finish. "Can I have a glass too, Grandma? I'm dying of thirst."

I could see Marissa through the kitchen's bay-window, standing next to her grandfather with her head down while he was yelling at her. The reverend and Carlos were having their own discussion at the end of the driveway with Fred doing his best to get Carlos to play.

"There's pop in the fridge," Bonnie said.

He looked disappointed, but went to the refrigerator anyway. "Hey, that was some explosion, huh?"

"It could have been worse," I answered. "Lucky for Lonnie the tank didn't burst."

"Yeah. Dad's gonna be pissed losing the barbeque. At least he won't have to buy a new tank."

"The grill belongs to your father?"

"It was nearly brand new when he lent it to Aunt Bonnie for the picnic. Only used one bottle of gas before I brought it up here last week."

The door opened before Alec could finish his story. Reverend Johnson let himself in. I could see Carlos out the window, throwing a stick for Fred. "We've got to get going, Ms. Jones," he said to Bonnie. "I want to stop by the hospital and check on Lonnie. Thank you so much for inviting us. Carlos has had such a great time."

"My pesor, Wevland," she giggled; evidently, the alcohol was finally getting to her.

He pretended not to notice and turned to her sober twin, "Are you sure you don't want to ride back with us, Margot? It's really not out of our way."

"Thank you, Reverend. No, I want to stay for a while. Bonnie can drive me into town in a couple days."

I saw my chance to escape. "Let me walk you out, Reverend."

Fred and Carlos were in a tug-of-war with the stick when the reverend and I passed the barbeque on the way to his van. "I wonder if I should call Shelia," I said, and tried to read his face.

"It won't be necessary, Jake. I already called her. She said she'd meet me at the hospital."

"Oh, I forgot. Lonnie said something about her getting involved in the church. I suppose you know her better than I ever did."

"Yes, she's been a big help with the children, a real saint.

"Carlos. We've got to go now," he yelled while extending his hand toward me. "It's been a pleasure meeting you, Jake. Let me know when the book is ready. I'd be happy to take a look at it if you need a second set of eyes." This time his grip was a little too tight.

Carlos accepted defeat, and let Fred keep the stick. He came over to us with his head down like someone who had just lost his best friend. Fred followed, trying to put the stick back in his hands as they came closer. The boy got into the van without a word.

Bonnie and Margot were on the porch watching and waving goodbye to the reverend. I waved back too, and started for home when I noticed Lonnie's Jeep.

"Bonnie!" I called out, catching them just when they had turned to go back inside. "What about the Jeep?"

"Charlie said he'd take care of it," Margot answered for her. She waited for her sister to go back into the house, and then came off the porch toward me. "You forgot the manuscript," she said, holding it out to me.

Her tone was soft and gentle like her sister's and she looked tired.

"Jake," she said and paused before continuing. "Do you know a good lawyer?"

"Why, Margot?"

"Charlie is going to sue you."

"What? You're kidding? What did I do?"

She reached down to pet Fred. I was sure it was so she didn't have to look me in the eyes because this was a first since I'd been there. "He says you're responsible for the tank blowing up. He says he can get Lonnie everything you own and maybe put you away too."

I laughed, and reached out to take the manuscript. "There's no way he can prove I had anything to do with that accident." I hesitated for a split second considering my next words. "You can tell Chuck for me it was no accident. I'm beginning to think someone is using me as the scapegoat for a failed attempt at premeditated murder. Someone tried to kill Lonnie, and I think I know why."

Margot turned so white, I was afraid her heart stopped. "Are you okay?" I asked and reached out to hold her.

"Must be the drink. I'm not used to it. Why do you think someone tried to kill him?"

I led her over to the bench by the barbeque, or what was left of it. "Before that thing blew up," I said, pointing at the debris. "Lonnie said he knew who was doing all the poaching around here. He didn't come out and say it outright, but I think he was blackmailing the poacher."

Margot squeezed my hand. "Well, that's a relief. I thought you were going to say it was Alec."

I let go of her hand and picked up a stick. "Alec?" I asked, throwing the stick down the road for Fred. "Why Alec?"

"He set up the barbeque, so I thought you might think it was him."

I laughed and watched Fred chase after the stick. "I didn't think he could make his own truck payments, let alone pay off Lonnie. No, it has to be someone with money, or at least someone who can get some money."

"Speaking of money, Jake. Don't forget Daddy's book. There's a nice bonus if you can get it printed with that pip Bonnie told me about."

I should have known twins kept no secrets from each other, so I didn't bother correcting her on the acronym for print on demand. "I'll start on the book tonight. I can't talk to Lonnie about the poacher until he's better, so I'll get right on it."

Fred had the stick and was coming back already. I was in no mood to play, so I asked Margot to thank her twin for inviting us and headed up the road to my cabin.

Chapter 3

I'm not exactly a recluse. I don't even consider myself introverted most of the time. However, it felt good to be home by myself with only my dog to talk to. Fred never once pouted or became sullen when I didn't speak, at least not that I know of. I suppose that's why I preferred the company of a dog or a good book over endless chatter. Unfortunately, the book I was trying to read would never make any bestseller list and I could see why no editor ever got past the first chapter of "To Peleliu and Back," by Raymond Lockhart.

To begin with, Ray's typewriter needed a new ribbon. The type was faint and almost illegible. He also used single-spacing and had a complete disregard for punctuation. It was almost impossible to tell when one sentence ended and the next began. I had my work cut out for me if I had any hopes of turning the manuscript into anything readable. That's when I decided to skip the process of transcribing and tried scanning it into a computer file using an optical character recognition program. That way I could use the proofreading program I used on my own work.

I had been reading by the light of a battery powered lantern which wasn't going to power my scanner so I took everything out to my motor home and started the generator. Fred seemed eager to follow and headed for his favorite tree, only he didn't lift his leg. He started barking at something in the shadows. I felt an adrenaline rush and thought about going back for my shotgun when a big mule deer bolted from out of nowhere and ran up the hillside.

"Thanks for scaring the piss out of me, Freddie," I said while starting the generator. When he didn't comment, I closed the generator cover and went back to my makeshift office. Fred looked like he couldn't decide to follow or chase the deer. Evidently his fear of the dark overcame his hunting instinct and he joined me in the motor home.

My first attempt at using the OCR program created more errors than if I typed the text myself. Then I hit upon the idea to scan a few pages and tweak the contrast levels before performing the character recognition. I used a multi-function machine that could print, fax and scan. It had the ability to scan ten pages at a time, so I spent the next few hours feeding the twenty-year old manuscript into the machine. I was somewhere around page two hundred when the scanner jammed.

"Son of a bitch," I yelled. "Margot is going to be pissed." I knew the jam meant the scanner had destroyed at least one page of her book. Fred ignored my outburst and went on with his dreaming. He must have been re-living the excitement of running after sticks and rocks. His leg was twitching and his eyes moving rapidly under closed lids.

I could hear the generator coughing like a chain-smoker and knew I'd either have to go out and switch over to the main gas tank or let it die. I was too tired and frustrated, so I gave up for the night about the same time as the generator.

Fred woke first, as usual, so we did our morning ritual and I let him out the door before getting the coffee from the refrigerator. The fridge wasn't working since my electricity had been shut off, but it was still a great place to store things because my little cabin only had one cupboard and that was full of expired can goods I had bought at the local dollar store when they were on sale. I watched Fred through the living room window while I started my camp stove. My cabin was one big room plus a bedroom and bath. The one big room consisted of a living room and kitchen. I could see out the front-room window from every corner of the house. Fred went straight to where we saw the deer the night before. That brought me back to reality and yesterday's picnic.

"What did Chuck have against me?" I said to my empty cabin. I tried to remember when he had become so antagonistic. Was it before or after I refused to give him the manuscript?

I might have stayed at my window all day thinking about the picnic and watching Fred follow the deer scent if not for my percolator boiling over. Making coffee the old fashioned way was tough. Now I knew why nobody used the old percolators anymore, but it was the best I could do until I could get my power turned back on. It made me almost wish I had accepted Chuck's offer. I gave up on the coffee and decided I better go into town and check on Lonnie, even though he wasn't really a friend or even a good customer. He wouldn't have been hurt if I had warned him about the leaking valves. The least I could do was to stop by and see him.

The paramedics said they would take him to Lutheran hospital in Wheat Ridge, so I tried that number first. The hospital desk transferred my call to his room. Nobody answered. It was just as well; Fred was at the front door and wanted back in.

"What you got there, Boy?" I asked when I opened the door. My question was more of a greeting for I could see it was a stick, until I got a better look. "Where did you find that?"

He answered by dropping it at my feet. I hadn't seen the feathers on the shaft when the arrow was in his mouth. Fred waited for me to pick it up, and then ran off the porch. Just like a wide receiver, he knew how far I could throw a stick so he was headed toward that spot.

"Not now, Freddie. I've got to go into town. I promise we can play when I get back."

Fred ignored me, or maybe he just didn't understand. For whatever reason, he gave up and went back to where the deer had been the night before. I decided I better go get him before he found the other half of the arrow. If this was a hunting arrow, it could very well have a razor-blade tip.

"Holy, Jesus," I said when I caught up with Fred. There was a large red-spot on the ground with the telltale trail of a bleeding animal heading up the hill. It had to be the deer we saw last night. I felt a cold chill go up my spine. Deer season was months away; not that it was legal to hunt anywhere near here. If it was the poacher who shot it, he must have been watching us last night.

Reason said to follow the trail backwards to where the deer had been shot. Maybe I could find the poacher's tracks or something he left behind, but Fred had other ideas. He was headed in the direction we saw the deer run. I decided I better follow him in case he should track down the poor animal. The deer could be bleeding or dead. Fred followed the blood tracks up the hill and I followed Fred. Eventually they disappeared and Fred lost the scent before finding the wounded animal. I was somewhat ambivalent about not finding the poor thing. I don't know what I would have done if we had, yet I felt bad that he would probably become some coyote's next meal. As a result, it was past noon by the time I made it to Wheat Ridge.

The endless construction on the C-470 interchange had traffic backed up for miles. My old Wagoneer didn't like the stop and go traffic and began to overheat. I had bought the Jeep soon after returning home from Missouri last year. It had seemed like a good choice at the time. The price was right and it had tons of room for all my tools, but it drank water faster than a hippo on diuretics. Its temperature gauge had been pegged for miles and so much steam was coming from under the hood that I had to pull over on the shoulder to let the beast cool off.

Luckily, I carried plenty of water, so I pulled over to the side of the freeway as far from traffic as I could get without rolling the Jeep down a steep embankment. I had to wait nearly an hour before I could refill the radiator. Adding cold water to an overheated engine is a sure recipe for a cracked block. It gave me plenty of time to think of who Lonnie was blackmailing.

Alec had never crossed my mind until Bonnie brought him up. It was true the kid didn't have any money, but his father did. The rumor was Jonathan was losing his shirt in his roofing business, but he always seemed to have money nonetheless. Whoever the poacher was had to have access to the barbeque and its propane tank. I couldn't think of who that could be other than Alec and his father. Then again, maybe I had let my imagination get the best of me and there was no connection whatsoever to the poacher and the accident.

Once I satisfied my Jeep's thirst, I squeezed back into traffic and headed straight for the hospital. A get well card or balloon wasn't in my budget. It took another thirty minutes to find the hospital's front desk. All the up-front parking spaces were in a paid lot. I had parked half a mile away and came in the back entrance to save a few bucks. That turned out to be a bad idea.

The path to the front was worse than a labyrinth. The colored lines that represented breadcrumbs led me down the hallways to doors that needed a badge to enter. I must have backtracked a dozen times before discovering the path to the front desk. This was one time I wished I wasn't so cheap. A couple dollars for parking didn't seem like such a bad idea after all.

"Are you family?" the woman behind the counter asked, when I requested Lonnie's room number.

"No, just a friend. He's probably in the burn ward, or wherever you put someone with bad burns."

She took it in stride and punched a few keys on her keyboard. "Two oh five. The patient elevators are down the hall on the left."

I wasted no time making my way to the second floor, then began to have second thoughts about coming when I saw his estranged wife. I recognized Shelia the moment I stepped out of the elevator. I had never met her; I only heard stories about her from Lonnie. He was one of those guys who couldn't keep his love-life to himself. The pretty brunette being consoled by none other than Reverend Johnson had to be her. She was plump, but far from the Weight Watcher reject Lonnie had described. I found her terribly sexy. What a fool Lonnie had been to leave her.

Shelia was wearing tight pink pants and a pink blouse that did nothing to hide her assets, of which she had plenty. For some reason she made me think of the movie, Pretty in Pink. Even the book she was carrying had pink bookmarks. I couldn't help but wonder if she would be interested in an unemployed computer programmer now that she had left him.

She turned toward me when the reverend looked in my direction and said something to her. "Bastard! You have some kind of nerve coming here." She was in my face before the doors closed on the elevator. Now I knew why deer stared at headlights. I was helpless to react.

"You killed my husband, you bastard! You're going to pay for this. I promise I'll make you pay." Then she slapped my face and stormed down the hall.

"Are you okay, Jake?" The Reverend asked. I had my hand to my face where she had slapped me.

"Yeah. More shocked than hurt, but what's this about Lonnie dying? The last I saw him, he had a few first and second-degree burns. Nothing they couldn't take care of in the ER."

"Let's go back into the waiting room. I think you need to hear this sitting down."

Reverend Johnson led the way and held the door while I went inside. It felt like we had passed through a wormhole into another dimension. The colors were a light yellow and antique-white with table lamps instead of the harsh fluorescents in the hall. It even had a real coffee maker in the corner with what looked like fresh coffee. I went over and poured myself a cup when the reverend excused himself to check on Carlos, who was watching cartoons on TV.

The homey ambience broke when I saw the cups were Styrofoam. "Coffee, Reverend?" I asked as an afterthought.

He hesitated as though I'd asked a Jeopardy question. "Sure, why not? I'm supposed to be cutting down on the caffeine, but what the heck. Is there any artificial sweetener?"

I picked up a couple packs of sweetener and a creamer, and then went over to him and Carlos. "So what happened? Why does she think I killed Lonnie?"

"The shock of the burns was too much for his heart," he continued after taking a sip and speaking into the cup.

"A heart attack? How is that my fault?"

"Not a heart attack, Jake. Heart failure. His blood pressure dropped so low that his heart just stopped working."

"Whatever. I still don't see why Shelia thinks it's my fault," I said, trying not to show my anger at being accused of something I didn't do.

The reverend stood up and put his hand on my shoulder. The gesture was probably meant to calm me down. "Chuck was here earlier. I don't believe it myself.

He's been telling everyone you should be arrested for manslaughter. What did you do to get him so riled up?"

His big paw had its intended effect, but it made me uncomfortable, so I moved back a step, forcing him to remove his hand. "I don't even know the man, Reverend. All I know is he thinks I've been taking advantage of Bonnie by doing unnecessary repairs on her house and he didn't want Margot paying me to fix the manuscript."

Reverend Johnson looked me straight in the eyes. I'm six-two, but he was taller and made me feel ten years old again. Memories of fifth grade Catholic school came flooding back.

"I better go find Shelia," he said. "Watch out for him, Jake. Call me if you ever feel the need to talk."

"As long as you promise not to make me say the rosary ten times," I said and began to leave. Then I had a flash of déjà vu. *Could this be another black-widow murder?*

"Reverend, do you know if Shelia needs anything? You know, financially?"

He had already begun to open the waiting-room door and stopped to answer. "No. She should be fine once the insurance comes through."

Chapter 4

The traffic going back up the mountain was a lot better than coming down earlier. My old Wagoneer breezed up the hills without once overheating. The normal hour drive seemed to fly by, though I was too engrossed in my thoughts to notice. Only last year my sister had been accused of murdering her husband for his insurance. That little episode had cost me my entire summer when I made the trip to Missouri to help her prove her innocence. There was no way this could be happening again; besides, how could Shelia know Lonnie would be doing the cooking at the barbeque?

Bonnie was standing in her front yard when I drove up the road to my cabin. We both lived on Columbine Circle; she at the bottom and me at the top. I had hoped to give her a wave and get on home. Hope is for the hopeless, or so they say. She waved for me to stop.

"Jake, did you hear about Lonnie?"

"Just came from the hospital, and I'm still in shock. Shelia is blaming me and I think she's going to have Chuck sue me too."

"I hope they don't try to sue me." Bonnie never was a fan of Lonnie's, so her remark didn't surprise me.

I shut off the Jeep before it overheated as I could see this conversation would take some time. "If Shelia sues anyone, it should be your nephew. Didn't you say you borrowed the barbeque from Jonathan and Alec set it up for you?"

"Oh, you must think I'm terrible, thinking about myself when his poor wife can't even get alimony now." She had her head in my window and her hands on my door frame. I wasn't going anywhere soon unless I could think of a good excuse to escape.

"Speaking of that barbeque, Bonnie, there's something about it that's been bothering me."

"Now don't go blaming yourself, Jake. It's not your fault. How were you supposed to know it was defective? That reminds me, don't leave. I'll run in and get those leftover hamburgers for Fred. Nobody had much of an appetite after seeing Lonnie's face all burned the way it was."

She released my car and started toward her house without waiting for me to answer. I saw my chance and started my Jeep. "I'll come by after I check on him, Bonnie. I need to talk to you about your father's book anyway."

Bonnie was back in a flash; once more holding onto the doorframe so I'd have to drag her with me if I wanted to leave. "I'm glad you reminded me, Jake," she said while looking at my door like she was studying its paint. "Margot would like her manuscript back. She said she would pay you whatever time you put into it."

It didn't take a genius to know why. "Chuck?" I asked.

She finally looked up from Jeep's faded paint. "How did you know?"

"I'll tell you when I come back, but I really need to check on Fred."

She let go of my Jeep for the second time. "Bring him with you. I'll fix us a little something and he can have some of those hamburgers." I took off before she could hold me and my car hostage again.

Fred repeated his act from the barbeque when I opened the door by jumping up to give me a big kiss. When an eighty-pound dog jumps up to greet you, it's enough to knock you over if you're not ready for it. He had me down on the floor and was licking my face while beating the open door with his tail.

"Whoa, Boy. Don't kill me. I'm happy to see you too."

Once I was able to get back on my feet, I went over and checked on his water, and then took a beer from my cooler. It was warm, but after the day I had, I didn't care if it was boiling. Fred had already forgotten about me and gone out to relieve himself, so I followed as far as the front porch where I sat down in my favorite chair to keep an eye on him and quench my thirst. The rocking chair had been a gift from Bonnie, who thought every writer needed one.

Fred checked every tree and rock in the front yard before deciding on which one to water. I was on my second beer when he finally joined me on the deck. "Any more deer out there?" I asked and poured him a little sip on the weathered deck boards.

He lapped it up before it had time to soak into the deck, then looked at me and started barking for more. My sister had thought it was funny when she saw him do it last summer, and my mother thought it was animal cruelty. Whatever it was, it was too late to stop. Fred had been sharing my beer since he was a puppy.

I finished the last of my beer and poured the dregs for Fred and grabbed Ray's manuscript. "Want to go for a walk, Freddie? Your Aunt Bonnie has a special treat for you, and no, it's not alcohol, but I promise you're going to love it."

He answered the only way he could. With a bark, then ran to the path between Bonnie and me.

Bonnie saw us coming and met us at the door. She looked grateful when I gave her the manuscript. "Thank you, Jake," she said while holding out some money in her other hand. Margot said this should cover your time."

I stuck the cash in my pocket without counting it. Margot had plenty; she married into a very rich family, so it didn't bother me in the least.

"Well, don't just stand there. Come on in. Dinner's getting cold."

She looked at Fred, who had been sitting quietly next to me like a trained guide-dog. It was a first — he must have known what was coming. "You too, Freddie. I have a special treat just for you."

"At least he should get off my back now," I said while picking out the broccoli and setting it aside. It was probably delicious, if one cared for the smelly vegetable. The dinner she put together was getting cold. Neither one of us had barely taken a bite despite the fact I hadn't eaten since breakfast.

She played with her salad, then put the fork down and replaced it with a half empty bourbon glass. "He actually offered you five thousand for it?"

I followed her lead and opened another beer. They taste so much better when they are cold. "Yeah. Then he accused me of taking advantage of you. Said I was some kind of hustler. Not his exact words, but that's what he meant."

"I hope you don't think he got that idea from me, Jake. I've always told everyone you don't charge enough for the wonderful work you do." Bonnie acted shocked, but her expression betrayed her. I knew in an instant she must have said something to her sister that she regretted.

"Can I get you something else, Jake? I've got some of that delicious casserole left over that Lonnie brought to the picnic." Her smile faded. "Oh, that poor man. A heart attack?"

"No. Heart failure. The good reverend made sure I knew the difference. Lonnie's heart just stopped because of low blood pressure. It must have been the trauma from his burns." I automatically glanced out the window to where the barbeque had been.

"I see you got rid of the grill already."

"Jonathan came for it this morning; he's such a sweet man. I offered to pay him for it and he refused to take a cent. Said he could write it off as a business expense."

I quit pretending to be interested in my broccoli and pushed the plate aside. "Not much of an appetite today. I'm sorry you went to so much trouble." I fought the urge to save my dinner for Fred. He was the best garbage disposal a person could buy, but Bonnie might be offended.

She chuckled and then took a long sip from her glass. "Greg hated it too. What is it with men and food that's good for them?"

Greg had been her husband for forty years until he died from lung cancer. Her eyes still glazed over when anyone mentioned his name. "Give a guy a greasy hamburger or pizza and you eat like pigs, or should I say dogs?" She was staring out the window where the grill had been as if in a trance. "I wonder what he's eating now?"

I thought she was referring to her husband until I saw Fred chewing on something. "That's not a burger. I wonder what he's got?"

Bonnie put on the glasses that she kept around her neck on a chain. "It's a snake, Jake!" she shrieked.

"Couldn't be, Bon, I've never seen a snake up this high in all the years I've lived here," I said calmly, trying to quiet her nerves. "Let's go see what Fred has found."

She followed several feet behind me, ready to bolt at the first sign it might be a snake. "It looks like it's from the barbeque," she said when we got closer.

"Let me see that, Freddie," I said and reached for the hose in his mouth.

Fred let me get close enough to grab it, then got into his tractor pulling stance with his rear-end higher than the front and his front paws dug into the ground. He started shaking his head back and forth, daring me to try and take it from him. I reached for a nearby stick and threw it down the driveway. Fred let the hose drop and took off like a jackrabbit after the stick.

"Looks like the hose from the grill," I said after picking it up. I wiped off the dog slime on my pant legs before handing it to Bonnie. "This was cut with a knife. Fred's teeth didn't do that, and the explosion would have ripped it from the tank, not cut it." The hose had a small cut, not enough to sever it, but enough to cause a slow leak.

Bonnie put on her glasses to get a better look. "Are you telling me, the explosion was deliberate?"

"Looks that way, Bon," I answered while watching her flex the hose back and forth to get a better look at the cut.

"Margot said that's what you told her right after it happened. She said you thought Lonnie knew who the poachers were and that's why he got killed. You don't really believe that, do you? This hose could simply be defective or cut when Jonathan unpacked the grill." She held it out for me to see for myself.

"Maybe I'm just being paranoid, but I think I'll hold on to this for a while. Margot said Chuck was going to sue me and the reverend said nearly the same thing at the hospital." I answered without looking up from my examination.

I probably would have let the whole business with the hose go if not for the sheriff's deputy serving me a week later with notice to appear in court. Shelia had hired a lawyer and I was being sued for the wrongful death of her husband. I immediately got on the phone and called my new brother-in-law back in Missouri. He was not only the best lawyer I knew, he was the *only* lawyer I knew.

Ira advised me to seek local council as he wasn't licensed to practice in Colorado and couldn't recommend anyone. However, he did manage to remind me of OJ Simpson and the consequences of losing a civil wrongful death suit.

The hose was the only lead I had to prove sabotage, so after hanging up with Ira, I went to my shed to get it. I realized it sounded like I was making excuses again, and the more I thought about it, the more I realized any quick lawyer would claim it had been cut by a sharp edge of the grill during the explosion. For some reason I thought of Mark Twain, or was it Lincoln, who said, "The man who defends himself has a fool for a client."

"How the hell can I afford a lawyer?" I asked Fred after finding the hose behind a pile of garden tools.

Fred must have thought I wanted to play. He grabbed the hose out of my hand. "Give me that, you mangy mutt," I yelled and chased him out to the yard.

I tried throwing the stick trick. He stood over by the motor home, ignoring it and daring me to come and get the hose. I knew if I tried, he would run away, so I turned around and went back in the cabin. I was just in time to hear my cell phone ringing.

I ran to the kitchen table, where I had left it, and took a quick look at the caller ID. "Hi, Bonnie, what's up?"

"Jake, I just got off the phone with Margot and she is pissed."

"Pissed?"

"She says you kept a couple important pages of the manuscript and is threatening to have you arrested."

"Arrested?" I repeated.

"For stealing. Chuck told her she should call the cops."

"Not now, Fred." He had tired of waiting for me and returned with the hose, dropping it at my feet.

"Did you hear me, Jake? I can't remember the last time I saw her so upset. I tried to tell her you wouldn't do anything like that. Would you?"

I quickly grabbed the hose, catching Fred off guard, and laughed at beating him at his own game.

"It's not funny, Jake. Chuck has connections. You need to take this seriously."

"Sorry, Bonnie. I was playing with Fred. That's why I was laughing." I avoided answering about the missing pages from her father's book.

"Hey, while I've got you on the phone, you wouldn't happen to have Jon's number, would you?"

"You think Jon took them?"

I had to suppress a laugh. Not that it was funny, but I knew Margot wouldn't turn me in for stealing pages from her book. It had to be Chuck that got her so riled up and it kind of made me feel good to hear it.

"No. You mentioned he was having a hard time finding help. I thought I'd see if he'd hire me."

It took another twenty minutes to convince Bonnie I didn't steal the missing pages. I never mentioned it was my scanner that took them. The idea of calling her nephew and asking for a job came out of nowhere; it was an epiphany of sorts to get access to where he kept his roofing torches and propane tanks.

I dropped Fred off at Bonnie's after calling her nephew and getting directions to his shop. For a guy who was supposedly having trouble finding help, he hadn't been too receptive to hiring me. It took some talking and eventually he agreed to talk to me if I could make it to his shop before the crews came in for the day.

The gate to Jonathan's roofing company was closed when I drove up an hour later. I found a spot half a block down on Santa Fe and walked back to the yard. I could see why he kept the gate closed for gang graffiti was everywhere.

This section of Santa Fe had always been on the fringe as long as I could remember. There was a time when it was a nice residential neighborhood, being so close to downtown. The few houses that remained were never meant for the rich like the houses further east on the other side of Cherry Creek. They had been built for and by the tradesman who built Denver. Now the few that remained were boarded up and painted with multicolored graffiti designed to mark the territory of the ruling gang. The rest of the neighborhood was fenced-in with razor wire to protect the commercial ventures that dared to stay. Amazingly, parking was hard to find during the day.

Most of the cars belonged to students from the Auraria campus several blocks up. The rest must have been the employees of local businesses. The contrast was striking. Parked between student's late model compacts were beat-up pickups and relics from junk yards; my Wagoneer would be right at home. I parked between two late-model imports. If someone wanted to steal or put their colors on a car with a spray can, my Jeep would be safe.

Jonathan met me at a side gate to his yard. I had called him from my cell phone when the buzzer didn't work. "Jake, good to see you," he said, extending his hand.

He didn't look at all like I expected. Unlike Alec, his hair was dark as were his eyes, and his build was much stockier.

"Same here. Hope I'm not putting you out," I answered, returning his handshake.

"No, not at all. Work's been a little slow lately. Otherwise, I'd be out giving estimates and checking on the crews. That's why I'm glad you called. There's a trick I learned selling cars. When business slows down, hire more salesmen. You did say you'd work on commission, right?"

I couldn't help notice the way he pronounced the word 'out' with a Minnesota accent. "Wouldn't have it any other way," I answered.

"Great. Well, come on in and I'll give you the nickel tour." Jonathan locked the gate behind us making me feel trapped.

"Must be a pain when the crews come and go," I said.

"Tell me about it. I feel like a warden lately. The guy I bought it from got the business from his father who inherited it from his father. It was a nice Italian neighborhood at one time. I've been looking at a place on West Colfax, but it'll have to wait 'till business picks up. The rent would kill me now."

"That explains the name, Giancoli and Sons. I didn't think someone of Swedish decent would choose a name like that."

Jon's expression turned suspicious. "How did you know that?" Then the eyes softened and his smile returned. "Oh, that's right, you're a friend of my aunt. She must have told you I was raised by my father. Well, here's some of the equipment you might try to sell for me. I don't bother with built-up roofing anymore. I'd sure like it if you could find a buyer for those roofing kettles."

Part of my sales pitch to get the job was telling Jon about my computer skills, which had led to him quizzing me about Craigslist and eBay. "I could always list them in the antique section," I said.

Jon didn't see the humor in my joke. He looked at me like Alex Trebek does when a contestant misses an easy question. "Why would you do that? Shouldn't you list them under roofing equipment?"

"Just kidding. Actually, I'll list them under multiple categories and in different states. Craigslist doesn't like it, but I've found ways to get around the software they use to check for what they consider spam."

Then I noticed sitting in the corner the reason I had come here. "Do those propane bottles go too?"

Jonathan shrugged his shoulders and began walking again. "You'll have to ask my foreman which ones. We don't do a lot of torch-down anymore and there's some that are so old he won't use em. I'd be glad to get rid of those."

He had told me all I needed to know by the time we reached his office. One of the bottles had to be the one from the barbeque. If I could manage to 'borrow' it, I would have all the proof I needed to prove the accident wasn't my fault.

"Come on in and I'll let you do a take-off for me to see how much you know about estimating," he said when we reached his office door.

I tried to think of a way to get away before I wasted time on something I had no intention of doing, but I had to wait for his crew so I went along with the charade. Jonathan showed me to an old drafting table with stacks of blueprints. I thought they had gone the way of the T-Rex. I guess CAD systems and computerized estimating programs were too expensive for him, or maybe it was simply the way Giancoli and Sons had done it.

"This one's at half-scale. You know what that means?" He asked, pointing to the blueprint on top. Then, before I had a chance to tell him my twelve-year old knew enough to double her measurements, he got a call.

"Go ahead and calculate how many squares are on the roof, Jake, and I'll give you the material list and labor costs when I get back," he said and went to his office.

He must not have realized his voice carried through the thin walls separating his office suite from the cubicle I'd been assigned. I didn't hear every word, but it was enough to tell the conversation was about an overdraft. It sounded like an irate employee.

He acted like nothing had happened when he emerged from his office. "That was the wife. Looks like I've got to leave early. You don't mind if we pick up where we left off tomorrow, do you?" I realized I'd never be playing poker with him.

"I was hoping to meet your foreman, so he can tell me which propane bottles to list. I'll also need to take pictures of the equipment you want to sell." I answered.

Jonathan looked me in the eyes for the first time. *Had I been caught already?* "Don't put an exact number in the ad. You can be vague about it for now, and Mario will give you a figure tomorrow. You can take your pictures then, and make sure you get here by seven before they leave."

I made some more lame comments while he walked me out. He didn't respond until we got to the gate. "Damn traffic is starting already," he said as though he'd never heard me speak. "Would you mind closing it after I pull out? You only need to use one of the padlocks. Mario should be here soon enough."

"No problem, Boss," I replied to his back. He hadn't bothered to wait for my answer. I didn't have to wait long before I heard the low rumble of a big-block V8. I watched with envy when he pulled out into the street and burned rubber with a sixty-three Stingray. I hadn't seen one of those split rear-window Corvettes since I was a kid.

"Tomorrow, my ass," I said to the cloud of blue smoke and went back inside the yard.

I went straight for the propane bottles after closing the gate without locking it as I'd been told. Without a key, the only way out would be a climb over razor wires. I didn't need a shave that badly. There were five or six smaller bottles sitting on a pallet and next to them were the rusted ones without overfill valves I guessed he wanted me to sell. Any one of those could have been the bottle that killed Lonnie. It was too hard to tell. All I remembered was that the paint had peeled away from rust eons ago, just like the pile of bottles in front of me. Then I saw one with a regulator and severed hose still attached.

I had seen security monitors in Jonathan's office earlier and noticed they weren't turned on. I looked around for cameras; not that it mattered. The security company had probably shut him off months ago. Still, it made me feel better when I didn't see any pointing at me, so I grabbed the bottle and headed for the gate.

Richard Houston

I heard the roofing truck pull up in the driveway before I got ten feet...

Chapter 5

I made it back to the stack of propane bottles with my pilfered bottle before the gate opened and a roofing truck pulled in. I had my phone out pretending to take pictures when a tough looking Hispanic walked over to me.

"What ya doing, Amigo?" he asked. He had a tool belt slung across his shoulder with a menacing looking roofing hatchet within quick reach. Two more Hispanic men stayed back by the truck parked at the gate, watching. They were blocking my exit.

"You must be Mario," I said, putting my phone in my pocket and holding out my hand. "I'm Jacob, but my friends call me Jake. Jon wants me to list this old junk on Craigslist for him. You wouldn't happen to know which ones go and which stay would you?" I said pointing to the bottles.

Mario took his tool belt off his shoulder so he could free his hand. Then he turned to his crew, saying something to them in Spanish. He must have told them to stand-down, for they lost interest in us and went toward the back of the lot where I could see they parked their cars.

"Ain't that where the guy found all those hookers he wasted?"

I looked at him blanking before it dawned on me he was referring to the Craigslist killer from a few years ago.

Craigslist had, or maybe they still do, a section where hookers would advertise their services. The killer arranged to meet them, then kill them.

"Oh," I answered now that the light went on. "Yeah, but it's also a place to sell stuff no one in their right mind would buy." I was thanking my guardian angel that my story went over. Although Mario was a good six inches shorter than me, he had to be ten years younger and probably a lot stronger. His biceps were twice my size.

"Sell em all, Amigo. Then that cheap ass will have to buy us new ones. He knows they ain't safe, but wanted me to use them on the job anyway. The mongolitos would end up blowing us all to hell."

"Mongolitos?"

"The retards who work for me. You can't smell the propane no more in those tanks. Dumb shits leave the valves open if they can't smell the gas."

Mario's crew pulled up next to us in a cloud of blue smoke. Mario threw his tool belt in the back of the old pickup and went around to the other door. "Make sure you lock the gate when you leave, Amigo. We don't want nobody stealing those old tanks." He laughed when he got into the truck. His crew laughed too, as they drove off, leaving the gate wide open.

I watched as the truck went down the street. The blue smoke replaced by a puff of white whenever the driver shifted gears. After the third puff, I went back inside the yard and found the tank with the severed hose.

I stood looking at it for a minute or two. The hose looked like a match to the one Fred found, but what did that prove? The thought of finding the tank had seemed like a good idea when I first called Jonathan, but now I didn't know if I wanted to pursue my sabotage theory. I had something much better. I turned the valve on the tank and took a deep whiff. Mario was right. There was barely a trace of rotten eggs. It should be all the proof I needed to show I had no idea the tank was leaking.

Bonnie and Fred were outside waiting for me when I drove into her driveway an hour later. The sun had already set behind Mount Evans. Fred had no problem recognizing me in the dim light and was on me before I could get out my Jeep.

"Looks like he missed you," Bonnie said. I bent down to rub his ears and his tail was wagging so violently, his whole rear was swaying back and forth.

"Thanks for watching him, Bon. I didn't want to leave him out after you told me about the dog catcher coming by the other day and I had no idea how long I'd be in town. I really appreciate it," I said while holding the door open so Fred could get in.

"Where do you think you're going, Mister? Close that door and come on in for a drink. You can't take off without telling me what happened down there to get Margot so upset."

"Margot called you?" I asked, closing the Jeep's door. "She can't be serious about turning me into the cops over a couple pages my scanner ate?"

"No. She's over that. Come on in and I'll get you a cold beer. You're going to need it."

I told Fred to stay and followed Bonnie inside as I was told, which was more than I could say for him. He managed to stick his big nose between the screen door and jamb before it closed and followed us inside.

Bonnie handed me a beer and then poured herself a glass of her Black Label bourbon. "You've been a busy boy today, Jake. Jonathan says you snuck back into his yard after he left and stole one of his propane bottles."

My finger slipped on the pull-tab opening the beer and missed self-amputation by millimeters. "I didn't steal it. I borrowed it so I could get a better picture. He asked me to list some old equipment on Craigslist. You need pictures to do that," I answered, staring at the blood on the top of my beer.

She looked at me the way my mother used to when I was caught in a lie. I felt like I was a kid again. "Is it the same tank that killed Lonnie?" she asked.

"I'm that obvious?"

"You are to me. I put two and two together the minute Margot mentioned the tank. That's why you went to see Jonathan. You never wanted a job, did you?"

I got up and went to the fridge and took another beer, then grabbed her bottle of whiskey. "Let's go out on your deck and watch the sunset, Bon. I think it's time I warned you about him."

"About who?" she asked, following behind Fred as I headed toward her deck.

"Jonathan," I answered while waiting for her to join me at the table so I could read her reaction. The light from the dying sun took years of worry off her face. If for only a moment, she was a beautiful young woman again. I broke my gaze and continued.

"I think he might have tried to kill you. The hose from the tank to the burners had been cut so it had a slow leak. Jon knew you wouldn't be able to smell the leak because he gave you a tank filled with old gas."

Bonnie looked at me like I'd used a swear word. "You've got to be kidding. Jonathan would never hurt me."

She leaned back in her chair to flip a switch on the wall next to the table. The amber glow of a bug-light flickered on as the compact fluorescent came to life and I could see she was upset. "People do strange things for money, and from what I see, he could use a lot of that right now."

"Really, Jake, I'm telling you, Jonathan would never do anything like that. I think this lawsuit with Shelia has you grasping for straws, and you know all I have is Greg's Social Security check. If it wasn't for his veteran benefits, there wouldn't be enough to bury me."

"What about the house? Didn't you tell me it was the only thing Greg left you that was worth anything? I assume Jon is next in line after Margot. You've never mentioned any children other than Diane."

Bonnie's eyes glazed over and her wrinkles became apparent under the now bright-yellow light adding decades to her face. "Diane would have been your age. She was such a beautiful baby."

My social skills were next to Himmler's when it came to saying the right thing when confronted with other people's grief, so I shut my mouth and waited.

"Our marriage had never been the same after the so-called accident. Greg turned to God and I turned to booze. Things might have been different if they had found the guy who killed her. People need closure. Twenty-five years and I still want to see him hang by his balls."

She paused to wipe her eyes with her hand. I wanted to hug her and tell her it was okay, but Fred beat me to it. He left my side and went over to lie by her feet. It seemed to help and she continued with her story after absentmindedly patting him on the head.

"There wasn't anywhere near the traffic on Upper Bear back in eighty-eight that there is now or we never would have let her drive these roads. She was barely sixteen and just got her driver's license."

Bonnie paused for so long I thought she was done, but then she sighed and went on, "No one in their right mind would try to pass nowadays, but it was rare to see another car then. At least that's what the other driver said happened."

"I thought you said the police never found the guy who killed her?" I asked.

"Not him. The driver of the car he tried to pass," she answered. "He said it was coming at her straight on and she swerved to his side of the road trying to avoid him. Then, according to the other driver, he came back to his side of the road which forced her into the creek."

It was difficult following her story. I chalked it up to her being upset that I had accused Jonathan of trying to kill her. "So the guy who killed Diane was trying to pass another car on the road and ran her off the road into the creek?"

"Yeah, down by Indian rock. You know the one that juts out where the old Troutdale resort used to be. Nobody hardly used seat belts in those days, let alone air-bags. Her head went through the window. Was in a coma for a week before they pulled the plug and we watched her life drain away."

She wiped her face again with the back of her hand, then reached down and ruffled Fred's hair. "I need to use the little girl's room. Can I get you another beer while I'm in there?" she asked, and left before I could answer.

Fred came over to me after Bonnie left. He put one paw on my leg and barked once, looking at the empty beer can in my hand. He had me trained well. I emptied the last dregs on the deck for him to lap up.

"Drink up, Boy, then we need to get going. It's been a long day for both of us."

Bonnie was back before Fred finished cleaning her deck. She handed me another beer that she had opened herself and sat back down. I looked at Fred and shrugged my shoulders. I could tell he wanted more.

"I took the liberty of opening it for you, Jake, before you cut another finger. Now where were we before I got all sentimental? Oh, the house."

I gave Fred another shot. It was more as an excuse not to look Bonnie in the face than to pacify my furry lush. "My point is, Bon, I think Jon wants you out of the way so he can get your house."

"There's nothing to get. Greg took out a reverse mortgage before he died. It pays all the taxes and insurance and gives me a couple hundred a month. Between their fees and interest, my equity is long gone. Nothing left for Jonathan or Alec once I'm gone."

I decided it was time to leave. I felt like a fool. I was sure she thought it was another excuse not to accept the blame for Lonnie's death. "Maybe Chuck was right all along; it kind of looks like I screwed up big time."

"Don't blame yourself, Jake. It was an accident, plain and simple."

I stood up and crushed my empty can before placing it on the table. "I was being facetious. I know everyone believes I'm looking for excuses, but I truly believe that was no accident. Someone cut that hose, and I'm going to find who it was if it's the last thing I do."

She started to get up. I put a hand on her shoulder to stop her. "You're a good friend, Bon, and I'm sorry if I upset you. Please don't mention any of this to Jon and tell him I'll return his tank after I get it listed on Craigslist."

Later that night, I did list the tanks and sent Jonathan an email with the link, but I had no intention of ever returning the tank. It was the only evidence I had to prove Lonnie's death was not my fault.

Chapter 6

Fred woke me the next morning barking and growling at the door. It wasn't his "I've got to pee bark." Someone or something was out there. I knew better than to let him out alone for he might attack whoever was trespassing, and in this state I would be at fault. I quickly threw on some jeans and a shirt, grabbed a leash for Fred then went outside to see who or what had made him so upset. There were two Department of Wildlife SUVs and a sheriff's truck parked in my driveway. The sheriff's deputy was standing next to the open door of my motor home.

"Mister, Martin?" he asked. I noticed he had one hand on his gun.

"What's going on, Officer?" It was all I could do to restrain Fred. He must not have liked the tone of the deputy's voice.

"Are you Jacob Martin?" he asked again. He sounded annoyed.

"Yes. What are you doing in my motor home?"

He looked past me without answering. I turned to follow his gaze. Someone was turning up a terrible dust cloud racing up the road. "Do you know anyone in a red Bronco?" His eyesight was evidently much better than mine.

"It must be my neighbor, Bonnie Jones."

Bonnie pulled behind the deputy's truck and jumped out of her Bronco. "Are you okay, Jake?" she asked while walking over to me.

The deputy wasted no time in heading her off. "Miss, I'll have to ask you to go back to your vehicle. This is a crime scene."

Bonnie ignored him and came over to me and reached down to pet Fred. "It's okay, Freddie. Aunt Bonnie is here. I won't let these mean men hurt you." Then she looked up to me, "I saw all the cops race past my house and thought you were hurt or something. What's going on, Jake?"

An officer standing in the doorway of my motor home spoke before I could answer Bonnie. He was holding a compound bow. "We found them, Al. Right under the bed where he said they would be."

The deputy's reaction was instant. He had his gun leveled at my head, holding it with both hands just like in the movies. "On the ground, Mister. Now!"

I saw his hands shaking and wasted no time obeying his order. I had no intention of becoming some rookie's first kill. "Bonnie, please get Fred out of here before Deputy Fife shoots him," I said before the deputy could cuff me. She seemed to sense my fear and backed away with Fred, who was baring his teeth at the deputy by now.

"Easy, Al. It's not like he's armed and dangerous." The other officer had left his perch on my motor home and joined us. I couldn't see his face because mine was held down in the dirt. Fred was trying his best to free himself from Bonnie and come to my rescue. I prayed to God that he didn't.

Al, the deputy, released my head and let me sit up. "You have the right to remain silent..."

"I've seen enough cop shows. Forget your speech and tell me what the hell is going on here."

"Shut up and listen... If you can't afford a lawyer..." I waited for him to finish. His tone suggested if I didn't, I'd be eating dirt again.

Deputy Al no sooner finished reading me my rights when his partner took over. "Is this your bow, Mister Martin?" he asked in a much friendlier voice. It was beginning to look like the infamous good-cop, bad-cop routine. However, I could see now that the good-cop was really a game warden, or as the insignia on his uniform read, a District Wildlife Manager.

"No Sir. I don't own a bow," I answered while watching a female game warden taking some antlers to her SUV. "I wouldn't even know how to use one like that. It's a compound isn't it?"

"If this isn't your bow, why it was hidden under your bed?"

"That must be where that arrow came from," I said it out loud and realized my habit of thinking out loud might get me in trouble this time.

The game warden removed his glasses and went about cleaning the lenses. His real partner had also joined us after putting the antlers in her SUV. She came up from behind without saying a word. I could smell her but couldn't see her, and for some stupid reason, I found myself wondering if game wardens were allowed to use perfume.

"What arrow is that, Mister Martin?" I think I was in the fifth grade the last time someone asked me a question in the way he did. I had tried to explain to my teacher, Miss Jackson, that my dog really had eaten my homework.

I stood up slowly so Deputy Al wouldn't get the idea I was a threat. "My Golden flushed out a big mule deer the other night and when he came back to the house he had a broken arrow in his mouth. It was right over there by the motor home. When I went to check, I found a pool of blood so we tracked it up the hill but never found it."

Everyone, except the female warden, looked over at my motor home. I noticed her eyes were watching me. "Take the cuffs off him, Al. We won't be taking him in today," she said.

Deputy Al looked pissed. "Are you kidding? You got the bow and the antlers. He even admitted to tracking down a kill."

"You're left-handed, aren't you, Mister Martin?" she asked, looking at my hands.

"What's that got to do with anything?" Al asked, belligerently. The other warden didn't say a word. It was obvious he knew his place in the pecking order.

"I noticed he favors his left hand. Even when cuffed, he pointed with the index finger of his left hand, and that's a right-handed bow." Then unexpectedly, she walked over to Fred and Bonnie.

Whether it was her perfume or female pheromones, Fred took to her instantly; he started wagging his tail and gave her his best smile. "Aren't you a big boy?" she said while scratching his head. I swear I saw his eyes roll back in their sockets.

I had been un-cuffed and walked over to make sure Fred didn't do something I'd be sorry for. "He's really a pussycat at heart. All that growling was just for show."

"I'll second that," Bonnie chimed in. She had been holding Fred on a short leash and seemed relieved that he didn't bite the warden.

"I'm Officer Bartowski," the game warden said, holding out a hand for Bonnie. "Julie Bartowski. I take it you must live close by?"

Bonnie switched the leash to her left hand. "Bonnie Jones," she answered, returning the handshake. "I live right down the hill from Jake in the two-story mine-shed. It's a little out of style now, but back in the seventies that style was all the rage."

"I should know. I was raised in one of those over by Bailey. My father moved us out there so he could build his own house. That was before they had so many restrictions."

Deputy Al must have tired of the conversation. "If you two ladies don't mind, I've got better things to do with my time than to listen to this chit-chat."

"Thanks for your help, Al," Officer Bartowski said without trying to stop him from leaving. "I'll let Jack know what a big help you were."

Bonnie went on like Al had never been there. "Sounds a lot like Jake. He built this cabin all by himself. I never knew anyone so handy. I think you'd like him once you get to know him."

The warden finally seemed to notice me, even though my eyes had been glued to her all the while. It wasn't that she was going to be on the cover of any fashion magazine anytime soon, but something about her had my hormones working overtime.

"Poaching is a serious offense, Mister Martin. Someone has been killing deer and elk in this area for their antlers and leaving the carcasses to rot. We got a tip on the hotline from a 'concerned citizen' that it was you and they claimed to see you shoot a deer with a bow up there." She pointed up my hillside to where Fred had chased the deer.

My property was at the edge of civilization. Behind me were five thousand acres of so-called park belonging to the city of Denver, and past that were untold acres of the Mount Evans Wilderness owned by Uncle Sam. I managed to turn my head up toward the hillside while my mind was still focused on her face and body.

"Lucky for me that you noticed I'm a southpaw."

She looked back toward me, flipping her red hair over her shoulder as she turned her head. "You're still our prime suspect, Mister Martin. Plenty of left-handed people know how to use right-handed equipment. I'll have the lab run the prints on the bow before I make any final decisions."

"You want me to come in for printing?"

"No, that won't be necessary. I checked you out yesterday. Your prints are in all the Fed's computers. I was impressed with all those clearances from DOE and DOD. If they can trust you with national secrets, I suppose I can trust you not to take off until this is over."

I wasn't sure if it was a question or not, but answered anyway. "Scouts honor. I promise not to fly off to Mexico anytime soon." I made sure to cross my heart with my left hand. "Not unless you want to go with me that is. I hear Cabo is fantastic this time of year."

Her eyes seemed to soften when she looked at me without smiling. They were mesmerizing; somewhere between green and hazel. "Are you flirting with me, Mister Martin?"

"No Ma'am," I answered. "I would never think of flirting with an officer of the law, but you don't have to call me Mister Martin. Everyone calls me Jake."

"That's good, Mister Martin. I'd hate to call Al back to cuff you again," she said as she headed for her SUV, but not before turning to Bonnie and winking.

We watched while she drove off with her team close behind making them eat her dust from our dry-dirt road.

Bonnie let Fred loose when Officer Bartowski was far enough down the road. "I think she liked you too, Jake."

When Fred gave one last bark at the departing caravan, I knelt down and rubbed his ears with both my hands. "You tell them who's the boss, Buddy." Then I looked up at Bonnie. "What do you mean, too?"

"Men. You are so obvious. You guys haven't changed in ten thousand years. I thought you were going to hit her over the head and drag her back to your cave."

"Huh? I hardly said anything. She did all the talking."

Bonnie laughed. It wasn't a response to a joke kind of laugh; it was closer to a chuckle than a guffaw. "What was that about Cabo? You think Julie didn't get it? "

"That's not a name you hear much anymore. Is it?" I asked. "More like the mid to late seventies. I think it was pretty popular about then. Don't you?"

"Are you asking me how old I think she is?" Bonnie was still smiling. It was obvious she was two steps ahead of me and knew where my mind was. "Well, she's definitely your age, give or take a couple years; and single too, by the looks of her wedding finger."

Fred wasn't the least interested in my love-life. He heard Chatter in a nearby aspen and took off to chase him. "Forget it, Fred. You'll never catch him," I yelled as I stood back up.

"Thanks for coming to our rescue, Bonnie. I'm not sure what Fred would have done to that idiot deputy if you hadn't been here."

"It's what friends are for, but I better get back to my kitchen. I was in the middle of starting breakfast when those cops went sailing by," she answered while giving me a hug. "You're one of the few people I know with a heart, so I've got to watch out for you."

The hug caught me off guard and I couldn't think of what to say. I simply patted her on the back, then watched her walk over to her Bronco and leave. "Well, Fred, shall we check on what's left of our motor home?"

Fred headed straight for the rear of the old Minnie Winnie. I planned to go inside first, but he had other ideas. He came back to me, barked once, and went to the rear of the coach. He was standing by an open cubby when I caught up to him. It didn't take a master detective to see the door to the storage cubby had been pried open. It was the unit directly below my rear bed. "You think you're pretty smart, don't you?"

He just wagged his tail and smiled. I had to bend down and give him a big hug. "Guess I won't be trading you in for a Collie after all, Old Man. Now let's go inside and see how much damage those Mounties did."

Julie and her partner had left all the cabinet doors open, and the mattress and its plywood frame standing up against the rear wall. Other than destroying my entry door when they pried it open, nothing else had been ripped apart. I put the bed frame back and laid the mattress over it before closing all the cabinet doors. Our motor home looked like the day we bought it. I didn't find Jonathan's calling card until I started making the bed and found a tar smear on the bed sheet. There was the unmistakable streak of roofing cement that must have come from a roofer's work glove; I would have never noticed it if I hadn't inadvertently turned the plywood frame upside down when I put everything back in place.

Chapter 7

I spent the rest of the day surfing the web looking for information on bow hunting and poaching. My DSL service had been cut about the time Xcel shut me off. Little things like that didn't stop me from using the web because Bonnie was close enough that I simply piggybacked off her wireless router. I wasn't really stealing. She had suggested that we could share her service when I installed it for her and that's exactly what I did when the phone company cut me off. I just failed to tell her.

I discovered there was a very lucrative market in elk and mule-deer antlers. Some cultures thought they had magical and medicinal powers and would pay dearly for them, and then there were trophy hunters who would also pay dearly — up to five figures for a large rack.

The devil in me wanted to run into town and punch Jonathan in the face. The bastard set me up. I needed revenge. Then my devil's alter ego convinced me to keep my cool. The scene was straight from a cartoon.

I was glad I didn't listen to the devil. Jonathan was not looking so guilty by the time I finished with my search. I also discovered that compound bows like the one Officer Bartowski found under my bed were very expensive. Considering Jonathan's finances, I couldn't see him throwing that kind of money away to frame me, but someone put the bow under my bed and he must have been wearing work-gloves that had been used to apply roofing cement.

My laptop began complaining about shutting down if I didn't plug in the charger soon, so I decided to give it a rest and take Fred for a hike on the crude trail going up the hill to the mountain park behind my cabin. It was one of the many properties owned by the city of Denver which were nowhere near the city. The hills were home to black bear, mountain lions, coyote, deer and elk. This particular park was miles from the city and surrounded by private property. Unless you were a property owner like me on the edge of the park, there was very little access. Fred loved it. We never saw another soul on our hikes and he could run loose without a leash or without me worrying about getting a ticket for letting him go. The only law we had to watch out for was the law of nature. It didn't take Fred long to break that law.

I was sitting at the top of the hill and resting on a large rock out-cropping. The view was fantastic. I could see Willie Nelson's old ranch in the distance and Mount Evans still covered in snow right behind it. Below me to the north, I could barely make out the traffic on Upper Bear Creek Road. I would have stayed there all day if Fred hadn't brought back his prize.

"What do you have now, Freddie?" I asked when he dropped what looked like a skinned squirrel. I knew better than to reach out for his find. He would grab it and want to play keep-away, so I pretended not to care and waited. He kept watching me for the slightest clue that the game was on. When none came, he got bored and went to get a drink of rain water out of a depression in the huge rock I was sitting on. His forgotten prize wasn't a squirrel, rabbit, or other small game. It was part of a much larger animal — a very large animal. I'm no hunter or wildlife expert, but I know bear fur when I see it.

"Where did you find this, Boy?" Fred had returned with a stick and dropped it at my feet.

When Fred didn't answer, I got up and began walking in the direction he had come from earlier. Fred led me to the carcass fifty yards away. It was behind another out-cropping ten feet off the trail. This was not a kill by another wild animal. Someone had removed its head and cut open its stomach. It had to be the work of poachers.

"Get away from there," I yelled when Fred went sniffing around the dead animal. When he ignored me, I grabbed him by the collar and led him away. I didn't let him go until we were halfway down the trail.

I sat down on a boulder and held his head between my hands. "Sometimes you act just like a wild animal. That's a crime scene up there not a canine buffet."

He turned his head back up the hill, then looked me in the eyes and smiled. It was a smile only a dog owner could recognize, but it was a smile. I ruffled the hair on his head, then checked to see how many bars were on my cell phone. It was as dead as the bear. I knew I had to call someone and make a report, so I got up and started back down the trail. Fred was smart enough to follow and not bolt back up the hill. We kept on going past my cabin and took the shortcut to Bonnie's, through my back yard and across a dry ravine.

She was on her back deck and saw us coming. "Well, if it ain't my two best friends," she said when we got closer. "You guys must be psychic. I tried to call you and invite you to dinner, but your phone isn't picking up."

Fred made it to the deck before me and was already getting his ear massage when I joined them. "Tell me about it," I answered, watching Bonnie pretend to kiss him on the head. "Why do the batteries always seem to die when you need them the most? Can I use your phone, Bon?"

She gave Fred a pat on the head then stood up. "Murphy's law. Grab yourself a beer from the cooler and I'll go look for my phone. I'm always leaving it everywhere except on the cradle. I hope that battery isn't dead too."

I did as she said and helped myself to a cold beer after she went back into the house. I could hear her phone beeping on the far side of the deck. She must have hit the pager button when she couldn't find it in the house.

"It's out here, Bonnie." I yelled. "You left it on the rail."

She returned with a sheepish grin and a fresh glass of her bourbon. "Kind of miss the old-fashioned phone. The cord was a pain in the ass, but I never once put it where I couldn't find it."

I held a finger to my lips in the universal sign of silence. "Officer Julie Bartowski, please," I said to the person on the other end of the line.

"Oops. I didn't see you on the phone," Bonnie said softly and took a chair close enough to hear my conversation.

"I need to report a possible poaching. I found a black-bear carcass today and it looks like some vital parts were cut off."

Bonnie's eyes grew wider by at least a centimeter when she listened in on my conversation.

"Yes, I know there's a hotline for this, but she was out here this morning and I thought… yeah. What's that number?" I didn't bother to write it down and waited for her to finish reciting it. "Would you please ask Officer Botowski to call me when she gets in? She has my number."

I clicked off the phone and looked over at Bonnie. "God, I hate bureaucracy. 'Sorry, you need to report that to the hot line.' I'd like to report her to the hot line. What the hell is wrong with speaking to a real person?"

"You found a dead bear up the hill?" Bonnie asked before I could say anything else.

"Fred did. It was all I could do to stop him from dining on it." Fred looked up at me at the mention of his name. He had followed Bonnie and was lying at her feet again.

"It's kind of early for them, isn't it?" she said while petting Fred. The traitor leaned into her to get an ear-rub, forgetting who his master was.

"You think I woke her up? Is that why she wouldn't put me through?"

"No, Silly. Bears. Aren't they still hibernating?" She got up from petting Fred and went over to where she had left her glass. "I need another. Why don't you grab another beer and come inside?"

"I don't think so," I answered going to the cooler as ordered. "I believe they come out of hibernation in early spring."

"Well, I want to hear all about that bear while I get dinner ready. You guys are staying, I hope? I made enough chili to feed a bear." Then she realized her pun and laughed while going into the house.

Julie didn't call, of course. I doubt if my message was ever relayed. I had even gone to the trouble of removing a battery from my motor home and bringing it into my cabin so I could charge my cell phone. When morning came and after I let Fred out, I looked up the hotline number and left my report about the bear. I was done with it as far as I was concerned. I needed to get back to work on my latest how-to book and then concentrate on finding Lonnie's killer.

Okay, so what if no one else considered Lonnie's accident a murder? It seemed they were all content to call it a careless accident and point the finger at me. I knew in my gut that Lonnie had been murdered. I just had to prove it.

I had been assuming all along that the killer was after Bonnie and unlucky Lonnie just happened to be at the wrong place at the right time. Was I wrong that the rigged tank was meant for her? What if Lonnie was the intended victim all along?

So far my list of suspects was Jonathan and Alec, Reverend Johnson, and Charlie Randolph.

Chuck didn't seem to have a motive or the means to kill Lonnie. He was nowhere near the barbeque during the picnic, but why was he so gung-ho to have me tarred and feathered?

The good reverend had the motive if what Lonnie said about Shelia getting more than religion was true. More people have been murdered for love than for almost any reason I can think of, and let's not forget the insurance. Money is probably second on the list of motives.

Which brings me to Jonathan. Was Lonnie blackmailing him? If he was the poacher, he had both motive and Alec had the opportunity, but that didn't make any sense either. How would he know Lonnie would be using the barbeque? Then I remembered Chuck had paid Lonnie to do the cooking.

There was no way Chuck could be poaching. The only time I saw him move faster than a one-legged toad was when he thought Marissa was in danger. He would never have the stamina to hike these mountains chasing game. I needed more information. Maybe Ray's book could shed some light on this enigma as it seemed to be the one thing all my suspects had in common.

There was no longer any need to edit and correct the manuscript. Margot had fired me from that job, so I skimmed through the computer file I had scanned until I found something interesting, at which point I would jot down some notes with the page number and continue. It was so interesting that I kept nodding off. I was sound asleep when my cell started ringing.

The cell didn't actually ring, I had it programmed to play some of my Beethoven favorites. This time it was the opening bars of the Moonlight Sonata, which hardly brought me out of my stupor. I tripped over Fred, who was asleep at my feet, in my haste to find the phone in the dark cabin.

"Damn it," I yelled while accidently turning the phone on by touching it.

"Jake? It's Julie. Is this a bad time to talk?"

Now I was fully awake. I realized I had been dreaming about her. This was unreal. "Ah, hi, Julie. Sorry about that. I stubbed my toe."

"I just got your message. What's this about a bear? You found a decapitated bear up there?"

I tried to imagine where she was. It was too late to be in her office. Was she lying in bed while talking to me?

"That and his private parts," I answered.

There was a long pause. I checked my phone to see if it was working, then I heard her speak. "They cut off the genitals?"

"And slit him open right up the front. I think they took some other organs, including the heart."

"Sounds like poachers. I'd come out there now, but I was in the middle of a dinner date when the office called. I'll be out there in the morning with my team. Could you call me if you hear anything suspicious in the meantime?"

"You got it, Boss. Should I use this number?" I asked, referring to the number on my caller ID.

"Yes. It's my cell number," she answered. At least I didn't have to talk to her receptionist again.

I tried to get back to Ray's manuscript, but couldn't. Even if the book hadn't been the best sleeping aid since sleeping pills, I couldn't stop thinking about Julie's date. It never occurred to me that she was attached. *Was the guy her boyfriend?*

Fred didn't have to wake me the next morning when he heard the cars coming up the road before dawn. I had heard them too and woke in time to see Julie out my bedroom window as she left her SU, heading toward my cabin. I frantically searched for some pants before rushing to greet her.

"Morning, Officer," I said when I opened the door. "Aren't we early birds today? Would you like to come in for a cup of coffee? It won't take but a minute." I found myself babbling again. I really wanted to tell her how terrific she looked with her hair pulled into a pony tail that was sticking out the back of her cap. Even in the dim light of dawn she was gorgeous — maybe not Hollywood gorgeous — more like Daisy Mae than one of those skinny starlets.

"I'd love to, Jake, but we really need to get to that kill. Would you mind zipping up and take us to it?"

My face must have turned as red as her hair. I quickly turned around and zipped up my pants. "Sure," I forced a reply. "Just let me grab a coat."

Once I had shown Julie and her crew the carcass, she sent Fred and me packing. Bonnie was waiting at the cabin when we returned. "What's going on, Jake?" she asked when we were within earshot.

I pointed up the hill toward the hiking trail. "Julie and her merry band of men are up there checking on the bear."

"Julie? Whatever happened to Officer Bartowski?" Her smile was bigger than the entire Cheshire cat.

"Come on in for some coffee, Bon, I need to ask you something." I walked past her without waiting for a response and went inside to the kitchen where I started rinsing out the old percolator. I noticed her smile had been replaced by a look of confusion.

She leaned against the kitchen counter, watching me start my camp stove and place the percolator over the flames. "I think they still make the best coffee. Don't you, Jake?"

I set the burner so as not to blacken the pot with its sooty flames. "Not really. A little too strong for my tastes, but it will have to do until I get the lights turned back on."

"So what is it you wanted to ask me?"

"Let's sit down, Bon," I said and motioned toward the table. "I had a few questions about your father. I got back into his book last night and a couple of things he said didn't make sense."

Her pupils doubled in size. "His book? How's that possible? Did you copy it?"

"Sort of," I answered sheepishly. "I scanned it into a Word document so I wouldn't have to type it all, at least most of it. My scanner jammed around page two hundred or so and Margot took it back before I could finish. It seemed like a good idea at the time, but say the word and I'll hit the delete button."

Bonnie laughed and pushed me aside to lower the flame on my camp stove. I had been so distracted with my explanation that I didn't notice the coffee pot boiling over. "Don't be silly, Silly. You are some kind of genius. I would have never thought of doing that. So what is it you want to know?"

Fred must have tired of listening to us. He was standing over his bowl and staring at me, so I got up to get him water and food, but kept on talking. "I know it's supposed to be a work of fiction. Your father says so in his introduction, yet it reads more like an autobiography. It's a story about a marine and his island-hopping adventures during the Pacific campaign of the war. Didn't you say your father did that?"

"Yes. He even won a purple heart on Peleliu."

"I don't know," I said after taking care of Fred and sitting back down. "Maybe it's because of the first person point of view. It sure reads like an autobiography. Anyway, did you know his protagonist was witness to a fragging?"

Bonnie had taken the liberty to turn off the stove and pour us each a cup. She nearly spilled hers. "Fragging? I hope you're not telling me my father was gay?"

"Shame on you, Bon," I said jokingly, "It's not what you think. Fragging means killing one of your own and making it look like an enemy attack. At least that's one definition. The one your father used."

"Daddy killed one of his own marines?"

I took the cup she was waving in front of me before she spilled it. After taking a sip, I continued. "He, I mean his protagonist, witnessed a murder. He saw another marine shoot their lieutenant in the back with a rifle from a dead Japanese soldier. Then he put the rifle back in the hands of the enemy and rushed over to the lieutenant pretending to help."

Bonnie looked confused, but before she could answer, Fred went to the door and started barking.

"Looks like the posse's back," I said on my way to stop Fred from breaking down my door. I checked the zipper on my pants then opened the door. "What do you think?" I asked the beautiful redhead. "Is it a bear?" I had caught Julie with her hand in midair, ready to knock on the door. One of her fellow agents was standing on the stairs behind her, I assume to watch her backside.

"Can we come in, Jake?"

I opened the door wide and gave a little bow while waving them inside with one hand and holding Fred's collar with the other. His eyes were all over Julie's partner and I couldn't take the chance he'd jump the guy to protect his turf.

"Does he bite?" asked the other officer, with a hand resting on his closed holster.

"He's a pussycat, Darrell," Julie said, "but I know how you are with dogs, so why don't you and John go back to the office? I'll be along soon." I could tell from her expression and tone of voice that she wasn't asking; it was an order.

Darrell mumbled something I couldn't hear, and then left as he was told. I took Fred through the kitchen to put him on the back deck.

Julie wasted no time crossing the living room and bending down to rub Fred behind the ears. I swear I heard him purr; maybe he really was a pussycat. "Don't you worry, Big Fella, I won't let that mean man hurt you," she said to him.

"Can I get you anything, Officer?" Bonnie asked. She had been watching the whole thing from the kitchen table and had a huge grin on her face. "Jake just made some of his famous burnt coffee."

Julie stood up and looked over at Bonnie. "Burnt coffee?" Then she turned back to me, "How do you burn coffee?"

Bonnie burst out laughing. "Cream and sugar?" she asked between chuckles. "I'd offer you one of those artificial things, but Jake doesn't use it."

"Sugar would be great." She gave Fred one last pat on the head and turned her attention toward me. She could have been the poster-girl for the Ireland tourist bureau; even her eyes were green. "It's definitely a poacher, Jake. Looks like you'll get the top reward if we ever catch who did it."

I wanted to ask how much that would be, but let it go. Bonnie must have read my mind. "How much is that, Officer?"

"Julie. Please call me Julie," she said, turning toward Bonnie. "One thousand dollars. Twice the normal reward for crimes this heinous. They took every conceivable organ you can think of."

"Why would they do that?" Bonnie asked. "Is it some kind of devil worship or something?"

"No. I don't think so. Those organs are worth a small fortune on the Asian market. They use them for everything from curing ED to arthritis."

I took it as my cue to get the coffee and went to the sink and rummaged for my cleanest dirty cup. "That's sort of what I figured too," I said while rinsing out the cup in a pail of water. "Just like the antlers, but I doubt if they'll be back now that they know Fred is here."

Julie had seen me at the sink. "I'll have to pass on the coffee, Jake. I really need to get going. My guys placed some game cameras out on the trail and another where the trail crosses the road. Hopefully the perps will try again and give us a picture of their license number."

I put the cup on the table and followed her to the door. "So do you believe me now?" I asked before she could reach the door knob.

She went ahead and opened the door anyway, but turned before leaving. "If you mean do I believe you didn't shoot that deer? I believed you yesterday, Jake. You're too sweet to do anything like that," she answered and winked at me.

I stood in the open door and watched her leave. The old tune from the fifties, What is Love, playing in my head. It had to be the ponytail.

Chapter 8

Bonnie was in the kitchen washing my dirty dishes when I closed the door and joined her and Fred, who was waiting by her side for any scrap of food she might find. "I think she took a shine to you," she said without looking up.

She woke me from my daydream. The lyrics from the old song still stuck in my head. "You don't need to do those, Bon. I was going to get to them sooner or later, and what makes you think she likes me?"

"I'm not so old, I can't see, Silly," Bonnie said after placing a dish in my rinse water. Then, without missing a beat, she changed the subject. "It would sure be a lot easier if you had some running water."

"It would never work even if she did like me. Women like her need to be in charge of everything. Before you know it, she'd have me eating broccoli and cauliflower. Besides, her job would always come first."

Bonnie gave me a knowing smile and put the last cup in the rinse bucket. She pulled a cigarette out of nowhere, and then must have remembered where she was. "I'm going out on the back deck. I know you don't approve of these, so come with me and tell me about my father's manuscript. You don't think you can just leave me hanging like that after telling me he was part of a murder, do you? Or is it some kind of joke?"

Although the day had been quite pleasant, it was getting late and the temperature drops precipitously in the higher altitudes. I took a light jacket from the closet and then grabbed the comforter off my bed for Bonnie before joining her. Fred didn't need anything to keep warm and was already lying at her feet.

"Thought you might want something to keep the chill away," I said, handing her the comforter.

"Thank you, Jake. You're such a sweetie. Diane would have loved you."

I didn't reply to that remark. Bonnie had been drinking the hard stuff most of the day, and I didn't want to go there. "It's no joke, Bon. Everything I said about your father's book is true. I mean, it's what I read, I don't know if it really happened or if it is a work of fiction."

She lit another cigarette and took a deep drag before answering. "Who do you think he killed?"

It was nearly dark now. My solar porch lights were beginning to shed some light, but not enough to hide the glow of her cigarette. "In the book it was the platoon leader. If it's not fiction, there should be a record of him as killed in action. I can check the archives if you'd like."

She was about to take another drag of her cigarette, but stopped. "Archives?"

"It's a government database with everyone's war records. They have a limited version online that I searched last year to learn more about my father after he passed away."

"Oh, please, Jake! I won't be able to sleep until I know. Daddy would never be part of something like that fragging."

We spent another hour or so talking about the little she knew about her father's war experiences. He had never been the kind to talk about the war, which was why she and Margot were so surprised when he wrote a book about it. I waited until she left for home before starting my search of the archives.

I didn't have much to go by. Bonnie didn't know what unit her father was in let alone his serial number. She did tell me he made it to corporal by the end of the war. All I knew was an approximate date and that the incident happened on Peleliu. The rest I had to tweak out of the internet.

Dawn was breaking when I finished a somewhat fruitless search, although I had a new respect for the Marines who fought the war. All the movies and novels I'd read never once mentioned how many thousands had given everything fighting for our country. The list of killed in action on Peleliu alone was overwhelming. Once I found that list, it took me the better part of the night searching for Second Lieutenants. Now all I had to do was get Bonnie to request her father's war record from the National Archives and Records Administration then cross reference my list of killed in action for his unit and company. Unless I was willing to pay a third party for the information, those records were only available by request from a member of the Marine's family. In the meantime, I needed to get Shelia off my back.

She would surely win her civil suit, and probably get a judgment for everything I owned if I didn't convince her that Lonnie's death wasn't my fault. Telling her it was murder might not be wise at this point. I still didn't have proof and there was a slim chance she was involved. I decided to simply explain his 'accident' was caused by a faulty propane bottle. I'd call her once I got some sleep, and hope she'd listen to reason.

I didn't believe for a minute that she had really been so upset over Lonnie's death. After all, she had left him over a month ago, so it had to have been a big act when she said she'd make me pay. I'd bet dollars to donuts Chuck had put her up to it.

Fred had other ideas, of course. He had slept through the night while I toiled at my computer and now he wanted out. "Okay. Okay, you scroungy mutt. I'm coming," I said and stumbled to the door fifteen minutes after dozing off. "If you don't learn how to use a litter-box pretty soon, I'm gonna trade you in for a cat." So much for sleep; I let Fred out, then went back inside to look up Shelia's number.

Her voice mail picked up on the fifth ring. "Hi, Shelia, this is Jacob Martin," I said after the beep. "I was wondering if I can come down and talk. I discovered that the propane bottle was defective and I'd like to show it to you. Please call. I know you must hate me, but I really had nothing to do with Lonnie's accident and I can prove it."

The machine cut me off before I could say more, which was probably a good thing since I tend to babble when I'm nervous. Fred was back at the door and I was finally going to get some sleep.

I must have really been tired. The sun had set when Fred woke me hours later. He was at the door again, only this time it was his intruder bark. Looking out the window I could see movement over by my motor home and the telltale dance of a flashlight. It was so dim that it was probably a penlight. Whoever was out there didn't want me to know. I quickly ran into the bedroom and threw on some jeans and a shirt, then stumbled around in the dark looking for my shoes. It only took a few minutes, but it seemed like hours. The intruder could have knocked down my door and shot me and Fred in the time it took me to get dressed. What was I thinking? My first reaction should have been to get my shotgun. Ten seconds later I had my twelve gauge and was out the door.

Once again, I was too late. I could see taillights on the road fading quickly as the intruder sped away. Fred was no longer barking. He was in defense mode with his ears back and the hair on his back standing up like a porcupine. He went straight for the back of the motor home. I decided to head the intruder off by running down the hill and catch him on the lower road.

With the flashlight in one hand and my shotgun in the other, I ran down the path between my cabin and Bonnie's. I didn't get ten yards before I stumbled over a rock and fell. "Damn it," I yelled when I saw I had torn my last good jeans. Then I saw the truck race by Bonnie's. I was too late and still couldn't get a clear picture of it or the driver. Fred had followed me and was now licking my face. It must have been his way of pretending to be a Saint Bernard.

With nothing broken or bruised other than my ego, I got back up and went back to the motor home. I swept the beam of my flashlight in a circle to make sure we were alone, and then let it rest on the rear storage compartment. I expected to see it pried open. I had replaced the flimsy flip lock with a padlock after they broke in and planted the bow. The intruder would have to break a much stronger lock this time, but it was still shut tight and locked. Then I checked the door of my motor home and saw its new lock was okay as well. Fred must have scared off the intruder with his barking before he had a chance to do whatever he was trying to do, but just to make sure, I went inside my motor home to check it out. I flipped the light switch by the door, and then remembered I had borrowed the battery to charge my cell phone. It probably saved our lives. The place smelled of rotten eggs and a spark from a switch or light would have sent the motor home flying.

I quickly ran over to the stove and checked the burners. They were turned off. The same was true for the furnace. That left the hot water heater or refrigerator. Both of which were accessible from outside. I was out the door in a flash and ran straight to the access door of the water heater. Sure enough, the propane line to the unit had been cut. I wasted no time running to the other side of the coach to shut off the propane at the tank. Now I just had to hope the gas would dissipate before finding a spark to ignite it.

Fred wanted to follow me back inside; he had been glued to me the entire time. "Stay!" I said when I re-entered the motor home. It might have worked if I could have shut the door to keep him out, but I needed to air it out, not turn it into a bomb.

"Why would anyone want to blow up our motor home, Freddie?" I asked while sniffing the air. I had opened every window and vent and was trying to decide if it was safe to switch to the engine's battery and turn on the lights.

"Or maybe it's not the motor home they were after. Do you think someone is out to get us?" Lights could wait, I decided. Tomorrow would be soon enough to finish my inspection. Calling 911 was out of the question. I had no proof that someone tampered with the gas line and my only witness couldn't back up my story.

My first thought after returning to the cabin was to call Julie and ask her to check on her game cameras. Maybe I'd get lucky. There was a good chance the one facing the road had snapped a picture of the intruder's vehicle. That would have to wait until morning. It was after nine already; far too late for her to be in the office. Then I thought about going into town to get something to eat, and quickly reconsidered. What if my visitor decided to come back and finish what Fred interrupted? Besides, the only restaurant open would be McDonald's. It was still several months before the tourist season got going. Only the bars would be open at this hour and their food was terrible. We would have to settle for scrambled eggs and sausage.

Having slept a good ten hours during the day, I found it impossible to sleep after dinner. Fred had no such problem; only a dog could sleep that much. Sometimes I really envied him. Bored and wide awake, I decided to get back to Ray's manuscript. Maybe that would help put me to sleep. I went back to the passage on the fragging to see if I had missed anything.

"I had gone off to take a crap when I saw him get it in the back. Sarge didnt see me squatting in the bushes with my ass all sticking out like that when he let the bastard have it in the back. I had to sit there and watch him put the rifle back in the hands of a dead jap and then walk off like nobodys busnines. Once he left and I new the coast was clear I got to shitin and gittin before he come back."

It was difficult reading to say the least. The editor in me wanted to scream, but I had to let it go and concentrate on the story.

"None of us cared much for the bastard too much anyways so we was all happy when he got it in the back he had it comming to him from the getgo and we was happy as larks to see him gone."

I skimmed over several pages describing the 'jungle thicker than thieves', 'humidity you could cut with a knife', 'mosquitoes bigger than crows', and 'latrines smelling like shit' before getting to the last of it.

"Mike and me made a pact that night to never breathe a word or let Sarge know we seen him do the bastard in with the japs rifle it was like making a pact with the devil it was."

There was more to the story, but this was all I got before my scanner jammed. Whatever happened beyond page two hundred was in the hands of Charlie Randolph. My chances of seeing the rest of the story were about the same as winning the lotto without a lotto ticket, but it was enough. I shut off my computer and went over to the couch with a yellow notepad to jot down some thoughts. I fell asleep dreaming about the scene in The Shining where Jack Torrance kept writing the same sentence over and over again.

I woke before Fred and immediately looked at my notepad from the night before. A sense of relief came over me when I saw no mention of Jack being a dull boy, but I had doodled a message to myself to call Shelia and

Julie. There was a crude sketch of a musical score with two sets of notes that I instantly recognized as the opening of Beethoven's famous symphony next to Julie's name.

Shelia had not returned my call from the day before, so I could assume she wasn't interested in my excuse about the propane bottle, or maybe she just didn't get the message. I tried calling again and went through the same scenario. After talking to her voice mail again, I tried Julie's number.

"Department of Wildlife, this is Julie Bartowski."

"Hi, Julie, it's Jake. Are you busy?" I asked before I realized I was speaking to a machine.

"I can't take your message at this time. Our office hours are nine 'till four-thirty, Monday through Friday. Please leave a message at the beep or press zero for the operator if you wish to speak to someone else."

I nearly sent my cell phone flying; I'd forgotten it was Saturday. *Didn't anyone answer their phone anymore?* This was supposed to be her private number.

My question was answered seconds later when my phone started in with Beethoven's Fifth. "Jake, what's up? Are you in trouble?"

"No. Just sitting here listing to Beethoven."

"Oh. I thought the poachers came back." There was a slight pause and a change in her tone when she continued. "How are you and Fred doing? I've been thinking about you two all day. I'm glad you called."

Thinking about us? Could I be that lucky? "We had another... uh, incident last night. I think someone is trying to do me in. It's nothing I can prove so I didn't call the cops, but your camera might have caught a picture of their car. I was wondering if you could let me see the pictures from around eight-thirty to nine last night?"

"How bout I drop by after, say around six? You still have internet access?"

"Yeah," I answered unwittingly doing my best Forest Gump imitation. Then it hit me. "Oh, of course, its wireless; you can access them from a browser."

"That's right, Smarty. See you at six." The line went dead before I could answer. I stared at my cell phone for several seconds with Beethoven playing in my head. I would never be able to hear his symphony again without thinking of Julie.

"Six o'clock, Fred. That only gives us eight hours to get this dump in shape and put together a romantic dinner." Fred cocked his head sideways. The mention of food always got his attention.

It took me all of two minutes to realize my plastic glasses and yard-sale dishes were no way to impress a lady. I had no delusions of trying to cook either. I would have to make a trip to Safeway's deli for our dinner, but first I needed to call Bonnie to see if she would lend me some nice china and crystal glasses.

Fred and I were knocking at her door twenty minutes later.

"You're a life saver, Bon," I said when I saw the package she had put together. There was a set of expensive looking dishes, gold-trimmed silverware, and very thin crystal wine glasses. She even topped it off with a matching set of candle holders and a linen table cloth.

"Nothing's too good for my boys," she replied with her famous Cheshire grin. "I could tell you really want to impress this gal."

She made me smile too when I noticed the joy in her eyes.

"Am I that transparent?"

"Like a teenager on prom night. You reminded me of my Diane when you called. She had wanted everything to be perfect for her prom date. I wish I'd known then I'd only have her for another week." Her smile vanished faster than Lewis Carol's cat and tears began to form in her eyes.

I put down the box of dishes and went over to give her a hug.

"I'm sure she's smiling at you now, Bon." I let go so she could wipe her face when I felt tears on my shirt.

"I was just going to open a new bottle of Jack Daniels. You guys want to join me?" she asked, forcing a smile. I made a lame excuse about not wanting to drink and drive because I had to run into town for flowers and food.

There was a very expensive BMW parked at the mailboxes when I pulled out on Upper Bear. I didn't give it a second thought even though I didn't recognize the car or driver. My neighbors along the creek bought autos that matched their incomes.

My thoughts were on Diane's accident as we approached the new Troutdale development when I noticed the BMW getting closer. I decided to let the other driver pass, so I pulled over at a short turnout. This had to be the place where Diane went into the creek. I was only yards from the rock outcropping that looked like an Indian to some and a duck to others.

The driver of the BMW slowed as he passed, then parked halfway on the road before walking back toward me. "Are you Jacob Martin?" he asked when he reached my Jeep.

"Yes," I answered, wondering how he knew my name. Then it hit me. He had been waiting at the mail boxes for me. His fancy car was too low to make it up our rutted dirt-road, so he had just waited for me to come to him.

He produced a piece of paper from out of nowhere and handed it to me.

"You have been duly served. Have a nice day."

I stood and watched while he left as quickly as he had come. My hand still outstretched and holding the paper he gave me. I waited until his car was out of sight before reading the summons ordering me to cease and desist harassing Shelia. I wasn't allowed within 100 yards of her and told not to make contact by phone, internet or any other means.

Chapter 9

My day didn't get any better after the restraining order. On the way back home, Julie called and said something had come up and she wouldn't be able to make our date. At least she said a date and not an appointment. She said she would call later and hoped I didn't mind. Fred didn't need any more people food so I decided to stop off at Bonnie's and share my dinner with her.

"Looks like something from a lawyer, if you ask me," Bonnie said when I showed her my summons. "This ain't no court document."

We were enjoying roasted basil chicken breasts with grilled portabella mushroom caps covered with herbed goat-cheese cream. I had found a new gourmet caterer in the Safeway shopping center that just happened to have a special on a canceled order.

I took a long sip of my forty-dollar wine from Bonnie's crystal, making sure my little finger stood out prominently.

"They told me Sauvignon Blanc had just the right acidic blend to match the astringent essence of our meal. You must give it a try, my dear." It was enough to make her smile again, but not enough to put down her Jack Daniels.

"Seriously, Jake. Stay away from that bitch. Pulling shit like this phony restraining order. She's trouble."

Fred didn't take his eyes off her. He sat next to her like one of those concrete lawn statues, waiting quietly for her to slip him another piece of basil chicken. Evidently she didn't care for the gourmet meal any more than I did. I had forgotten to mention to her that he was on a no people-food diet.

"I should have never stopped," I said while looking scornfully at Fred. "He served me when I pulled over across from Troutdale."

She reached for a coaster from the far side of the table, then sat her glass on it. "Troutdale? Why did you stop there?"

"I wanted to see the scene of the crime close up, Bon. I know it's changed since they tore down the old resort, but I needed to see it anyway. You know, to get a feel of it."

She picked up her glass again and held it with both hands as though the cold liquid would give her some warmth. She was looking at me, but I could see by the vacant look on her face that she was somewhere else. It didn't take a genius to know where that somewhere was. "I've got some news clippings in her hope chest. Let me go get them for you," she said, getting up. This time she set her glass on the kitchen counter on her way to an upstairs bedroom.

My statue came to life after Bonnie left. He was at my side begging before she was out of sight. It was my turn to feed him, but not before lifting my wine glass and wiping up the water ring it had made. I had been so upset about the summons that I completely forgot how much she cared for her antique table.

"You've got to be the best composter on the market, Freddie," I said, watching him gulp down the now-cold meal. "How can you eat that?" The sense of smell, they say, plays a great part in how humans perceive something will taste. The chicken smelled and tasted a whole lot better when it was hot. Now it was quite bitter.

Fred was licking his lips for more when Bonnie returned. She looked down at the makeshift coaster I'd made from another napkin, and smiled.

"Thank you, Jake," she said. Then, before I could say you're welcome, she continued, "We kept everything we could find on the accident. It's all in this shoebox. Got some pictures in there too." She pushed her whiskey aside and very gently placed the box on the table between us.

"Pictures?" I asked, watching her open it and begin pulling out yellowed newspaper clippings.

"Greg took them. He was obsessed with finding the driver. He thought he might be able to use pictures of the accident if they ever found the creep that ran Diane off the road." She laid the news clippings on the table and went back to the box, flipping through a stack of old Polaroids. "Here's one. It shows where she was hit."

"Not much more than a scrape, Bon, but I guess it was enough to make her leave the road."

"And here's a close-up. You can't see it now, but the other car must have been a dark blue."

"I'll take your word for it," I said, holding up the faded Polaroid to the light. I put the picture back on the table after trying to spot the blue paint without success. Then I selected one of the news clippings at random. It looked to be from the forties about some movie stars standing next to a big Duisenberg. A Troutdale valet was holding the door for a stunning blonde whose long hair covered one eye.

"That's Veronica Lake, Jake. She was huge back then."

"I'm surprised she can see with only one eye," I joked.

"They called it a peek-a-boo in the forties. Some stars still use it. I don't know what they call it now."

"Why the old resort, Bon?" I asked, putting the clipping back.

"Huh? Oh, you mean why did Greg keep those old pictures of Troutdale? He wanted pictures he couldn't get from the road. They had the place fenced in so trespassers couldn't get in, not that it stopped the squatters." She reached into the box, looking for something.

"Here it is. Squatters Caught Vandalizing Old Resort," she read aloud before handing me a newer article.

"Squatters?" I asked.

"Greg thought they might have seen something. He tried to track em down, but they were gone by then."

The caption below the pictures identified a long-haired boy with a tie-dyed shirt and his similarly dressed girlfriend as Robert Folsom and Linda Harkley. It said they were being arrested for vandalism and vagrancy.

"Vagrancy? There's a charge one doesn't hear any more," I said.

Bonnie rummaged through the box and came up with another clipping on the couple.

"They only did it to scare them. Greg said the vandalism charge was for a hole in the fence, and the cops couldn't prove they made it. See here. The parents are picking them up at juvie. They ran away again before he could talk to them." She flipped pictures and cards aside like she was searching for something important.

"And here's another picture of the accident. Greg thought it was strange that the only damage to her car before she hit the tree was that scrape." Diane's car was squashed from the front bumper to the front seats.

I took a quick glance, then put it back in the shoe box and reached for the lid.

"Are you sure the blue-paint scrape was made during the accident?"

"Now you sound like the cops," she answered, pulling the shoe box to her chest. "They said the same thing and wouldn't even look for another driver."

"I'm sorry, Bon. I didn't mean to bring back bad memories, but for the record it is entirely possible to push another car out of control with a small bump. I see it in police chases all the time on TV."

My statement made me laugh. "I mean I used to watch it on TV. Thanks to Xcel, I now do a lot more reading and writing without wasting my time watching the tube."

She didn't laugh at my joke, but it seemed to put her more at ease.

"Thanks for believing me, Jake. I was beginning to think me and Greg were the only ones who thought it was a hit and run, and now it's only me."

I picked up my now warm wine and downed it, then nudged my sleeping dog with my foot. It was time to leave.

"Can I take those with me, Bon?" I asked, pointing to the shoebox. "Unless those two fell off the edge of the earth, there's got to be some record of their whereabouts." I didn't bother with the leftovers. Although Fred would eat anything, it was too rich for him or me, but I did take my forty-dollar wine.

There was a record of the vagrant teenagers; over a million records. I found two million for Robert but only twenty-three thousand for Linda when I searched the web later that night. Because there were fewer hits for her, it took much longer to find them. Women have a bad habit of changing their last names. I had to search marriage records then search for all the different Linda Harkley's using their new names.

I started calling the list of six locals the next morning. "Hi, is this the Grabowski residence?" I asked after the third call. The first one had been picked up by voice mail and the second thought I was trying to sell her something.

"Do I know you?" It was a woman's voice, neither loud nor soft, but guarded.

"No, but I'm sure you heard of my client, Bonnie Jones. She has hired me to put some closure to her daughter's accident before she dies."

The line went as quiet as a phone line can without going dead. "The one on Upper Bear? My God that was so long ago. How the hell did you find me?"

"I checked the marriage licenses issued in Colorado for Linda Harkley and saw you married James Grabowski about ten years ago. Good thing you didn't get married in Vegas or I'd still be searching."

"I should've changed it back years ago," she said. "The bastard don't even pay his child support." There was another long pause before she spoke again. "Is there anything in it for me? This shit they give you for welfare don't buy much now days, you know."

"How about some pictures of dead presidents?" I asked while wondering where I would get the money. The last cash I had was the hundred Margot had given me for not working on her book. I spent that on Julie's dinner.

"What the hell do I want them for? Bring cash or don't bother."

"Cash it is. Can I come and see you tomorrow, Linda?" I couldn't get Jackson's pictures until Monday, but I didn't try that metaphor on her again. I crossed my fingers hoping she would wait until then.

"Hell, yes. Just make sure you bring frigging cash. I don't want no checks or pictures."

"Hey, Fred, old friend, how about lending your master a hundred bucks?" I asked Fred after hanging up with Linda.

When Fred didn't give me the money, I decided to walk down to the mailboxes. I needed the fresh air to think, and there was always the slim chance one of my publishers finally got around to send me my royalties.

Fred and I took the long way down the hill. I didn't want to run into Bonnie. I was afraid I might tell her what I was up to and mention the bribe. I knew she would be good for it, but it didn't feel right. This was something I wanted to do for a friend. Taking money would make it just another job.

I soon forgot about Linda when Fred came back with another stick. I threw it for him and let my mind wander to the propane tank and hose. My effort to tell Shelia the so-called accident wasn't my fault had backfired in a restraining order. I knew there had to be more to it. I could understand if Johnson was behind it, assuming they were lovers, but this looked more like the work of Charlie Randolph. *Why was he out to get me?*

Fred gave up with the stick by the time we made it to Bear Creek. There was a small pond with some ducks that were far more interesting than any stick. I left him to go swimming and crossed over our little bridge to the mail boxes.

There was a letter from Xcel and another from CenturyLink. They were both marked 'Last Notice'. To my surprise, there was also a check waiting for me. It was for an article I had written nearly a year ago. It wasn't enough to get the lights turned back on, but at least I could buy Fred some dog food with what would be left over after paying off Linda.

I was headed down I-70, headed for Lakewood, first thing Monday morning. I had made a pit-stop at the bank to cash the royalty check I'd received in Saturday's mail. I winced when it dawned on me that half of it would be going to Linda. It took me over a week to write the article and now she would get half the fruits of my labor for a few minutes of her time. Fred stayed back to guard the fort.

Linda lived a few blocks east of Federal in what was once a nice neighborhood. Now it was taken over by drug dealers, Asian gangs and junkies. I felt my Jeep was safe. It fit right in. Still, I thought better about locking it. The only thing of value inside the Jeep was an aftermarket stereo the previous owner had installed. If someone wanted it, they wouldn't think twice about breaking a window to get to it. I decided to take that chance and locked it before heading toward Linda's apartment.

Her building was a two-story cube. It must have been built in the fifties when the style was utilitarian cheap. The only embellishment to the building in all those years was the addition of bars on the lower windows. Her apartment was on the second floor, accessible from an interior foyer. All the mail box doors embedded in the wall had been torn off and the place smelled so bad I wanted to vomit. I rang her bell, and when that didn't work, banged on the door.

"You got the money?" were the first words out of her when she opened the door.

"That depends," I answered, fanning the five twenties I'd got from the bank. "Tell me something I don't already know and it's all yours."

She turned and walked away from the door, leaving it open.

"Can barely buy diapers with that anymore. Come in anyways. I'll tell you about the Corvette and then you can get your sorry ass out of here before Johnnie comes back."

I took a look behind the door and quickly surveyed the apartment for her Johnnie holding a baseball bat. Maybe I'd seen too many crime shows.

"Johnnie? I thought you said you had to go to work when I spoke with you yesterday?"

A baby started to cry from another room before she could answer. She hurried off without saying a word. My first thought was to go back outside and puke. The place stunk worse than the lobby. Over the stench of cat pee and used diapers, I could nearly taste a sweeter smell I recognized from my youth.

Linda was back before I could change my mind. She had a cute little dark-skinned boy clinging to her and suckling an exposed breast.

"He was driving a shinny Corvette," she said while patting the baby's back. "I knew it was a vette cause Bobby told me. We would've told the cops, but they never asked. Just hauled our asses off to juvie and called our parents."

I had a flashback to Jonathan's Corvette burning rubber down Santa Fe Street.

"Do you remember if it had a split rear-view window?"

"What the hell's that?"

"Was it a hardtop or convertible?"

She shifted the baby on her hip.

"Oh. No. I think it had a hard top." The baby now had her other breast exposed.

"Do you remember if the back window was one piece or two?" I asked, trying to look elsewhere.

"Christ sake, I don't remember. Can I have my money now?"

The baby had had his fill and started to squirm. I wanted to leave before he decided to dirty another diaper in my presence.

"One more question," I said while holding out the five twenties. "Do you remember what color the car was?"

She grabbed the money before answering.

"Black, I think. No, wait. A real dark blue. I remember now cuz Bobby said it was a bitchin' Daytona-blue and had to explain to me what that was."

I got out of there before Johnnie could come back and hit me over the head with his baseball bat. Linda had told me enough; Jonathan's Corvette was yellow, but it could have been painted over several times since the accident.

Instead of going west toward home when I hit the Sixth Avenue freeway, I went toward Denver. It ended by Kalamath and that was only a block from Santa Fe. The gate to Jonathan's yard was open so I drove in and parked right next to his Corvette. He was locking his office when I got out of my Jeep.

"Didn't think you'd show your face around here. You come back to return my propane bottle?" He asked while walking over to me.

I made a quick sweep of the yard before answering, just in case he wasn't alone. I still had time to hop back into my Jeep and make a run for it.

"I didn't steal it," I answered, trying to read his face. "I needed to get some pictures so I could list it on Craigslist for you. I sent you an email."

"My router's down. Haven't read any emails in a week." He seemed a little less hostile. "Get any response from it? I need to get rid of those kettles. Got a payroll coming up."

"No. I put your email in the ad and opted out of them replying to me. I also put your phone number so they can contact you that way too." I had thought about making a gesture of paying for the bottle, but changed my mind at the mention of his router being down. I knew from experience it meant he didn't pay the bill and I was afraid he'd accept my offer.

He studied my face a few seconds before answering. "Hey, I gotta go. We'll talk about this later when you return my bottle."

I couldn't let him get away without doing what I came for. "I wouldn't if I was you, Jon." I said pointing under the Corvette. "You better check your fluids before you go blowing a six thousand dollar motor."

He was halfway in the car by the time I finished talking. I didn't wait for him to answer and went to the front, placing my hands on the hood.

"Why don't you pop the hood and I'll check it for you?"

My bluff worked and I heard the latch click open. I opened the hood in record time and went straight to the radiator cap. It was all I needed. I could see the fender wells and firewall still had their original Daytona-blue paint.

"I don't see anything," he said from behind me.

I replaced the cap and then checked the oil. He was watching me now. "Looks good here too. Must have been a reflection."

He got between me and his car then shut the hood. "What was that all about, Jake?" he asked.

Evidently my subtle subterfuge wasn't so clever. It was time to come clean. "I'm trying to help your aunt track down the guy who ran Diane off the road, Jonathan. I just found out he was driving a Daytona-blue Corvette, just like this used to be before someone repainted it."

His hesitation suggested I hit a nerve. Was he trying to hide something or just scanning years of memory microfiche? "My God. Do you think it could be Lonnie?"

"No," I answered. "He told me he didn't get it until recently, when his uncle died."

Jonathan must have found the memory he'd been searching for. "That's true. He didn't own it until last year, but I remember his uncle let Lon use it on prom night."

"Prom night? Then he probably had a date." I said.

Jonathan actually smiled for the first time in the short time I knew him. It wasn't a nice smile. "You bet your ass he did. He married her six months later when her belly showed what they had been up to."

"That's fantastic, Jon. Do you know her name?"

"Does the name Shelia ring any bells?"

Chapter 10

Julie's state owned SUV was in my driveway when I got home. She was playing catch with Fred using a stick. I stayed by my Jeep and watched the show. I know they saw me, but they were having too much fun to stop. She gave the stick one last throw and came over to greet me.

"He never gets tired of chasing sticks, does he?" she asked.

I tried to think of a funny reply and came up short. She had been all I had thought about coming up the mountain and now here she was. "He's better than a boomerang, if you don't mind it coming back wet and slimy." It sounded so stupid once I said it. Why couldn't I come up with something witty that would make her fall head over heels for me?

She wiped her hand on her pants and smiled. "I'm glad I caught you, Jake. I came up to check on my cameras. The one by the road has stopped talking to the server, so I thought I'd stop by. You're not mad at me about our date, I hope?"

"Not if you show me those pictures from your camera. Why don't you grab your laptop and come on in? I promise we won't bite."

"I know he won't," she said. "It's you I worry about, Jake," she answered with a big smile before going to fetch her computer.

I gave her the deluxe tour of the place when she came back with Fred on her heels. That took all of two minutes. She could see everything except the bedroom without moving a foot.

"For some reason my fridge won't run without electricity," I said when I saw her looking at the kitchen. "Hope you don't mind your beer warm? It's all part of an article I'm writing."

"I didn't know you were a writer, Jake. What's the article about?" she asked while taking a seat at my table. "And as wonderful as that warm beer sounds, I'll have to pass. I've got a long drive home."

"Living off the grid; I'll have the lights turned back on once I finish the article. It's the reason for all the candles and camp stove." I paused when she looked over at my stove.

"I'm sorry I missed our date. It's been a while since I've seen anyone cook on one of those."

"Actually, I sort of had it catered. You missed a great gourmet meal, but I did save some of the wine I bought. It's not often I spend half my life's savings on wine, so you've got to try it," I said and went to the cooler to get it.

She laughed at what sounded like a bad joke. Little did she know I wasn't joking. At least she didn't object when I poured the wine in one of my few clean coffee cups. I had already returned Bonnie's crystal.

"So that's why the router is named Bonnie. You're hijacking your neighbor's router."

I could feel my cheeks burning. "Only until I get my lights turned back on, but I'm not really stealing. It was her idea so I wouldn't run up my cell phone bill." Of course the last part was a lie. Bonnie still had no idea what I was doing.

Her eyes never left mine. I had to look away. "Are you sure about the time of that picture?" I asked, trying to change the subject.

She had logged into her website during the time I was making excuses. "It's the day after I set it up. Lucky we downloaded a picture before it died. That picture is roughly the time you said, and that is definitely a vehicle," she answered while rubbing her empty cup.

I reached over and refilled her wine. "Too bad it's the only one you got before it stopped transmitting. With all that glare coming from the taillights and license plates, I can barely make it out. What are those spots? Is the lens dirty?"

"That's one of the reasons I came up here. It looks like the lens needs to be cleaned. It's also one of the problems with infrared. Reflections get blown out of proportion." She held up a hand in the universal sign to stop. "I've got to drive, Jake. Better go easy on that."

I added a few more ounces to her glass and switched to mine. "You can always crash here tonight."

She pushed her glass aside and looked up from the screen. Although it was only a second before she spoke, it was a long enough pause to make a point.

"Is that a proposition, Mister?"

I didn't back down this time and returned her stare. "I'd never think of taking advantage of a damsel in distress, M'lady," I answered, although the thought did cross my mind. "No, Fred and I will sleep in the motor home."

She smiled flirtatiously and reached for her cup. "In that case, Sir Lancelot, I will have more of this wonderful wine." She lifted the cup to her lips without taking her eyes from mine.

I refilled her cup when she set it back on the table, then as nonchalantly as I could, changed the subject. "Any way to get a number off that plate?" I asked while pointing to her computer screen.

She had won her staring game and knew it. "Maybe in the morning," she said and clicked the power down button, then grabbed me by the front of my shirt and pulled me to her.

"You like her too, don't you?" I asked Fred while we watched Julie drive off the next morning. I was missing her already and Fred knew it. I knew he knew because he lay on the porch watching her instead of Chatter who was teasing him from a nearby spruce. I knew it was serious when I picked up a stick and waved it in his face. He didn't budge.

"Come on, Freddie. Let's go check those cameras for Julie," I said and threw the stick down the drive past the motor home. Instinct took over and he was running down the drive after the stick before I had a chance to shut my cabin door.

Julie didn't have time to check her camera. I had made breakfast while she got ready for work and couldn't resist giving her a kiss on top of her head when I put the plate of scrambled eggs in front of her. That kiss turned into much more, which in turn made her get dressed all over again. Checking the camera for her was the least I could do so she wouldn't be late for her staff meeting. Well, maybe it wasn't the least I could do. I could have told her about Jonathan.

Telling Julie what I knew about Jonathan's need for money might get back to Bonnie. I had to make sure it was him before I said anything to anyone. Any good lawyer would say the roofing tar left by the intruder who planted the bow was at the most circumstantial. I needed a lot more than that to make the connection stick. Besides, if he was the poacher, then he probably killed Lonnie too. Bonnie would never speak to me again if I started shooting off my mouth that her nephew was a murderer. It was different when I accused him of trying to kill her. She knew I was looking out for her, but suggesting he killed Lonnie would be going too far.

It was a dilemma I had been tossing around in my mind all night after Julie fell asleep. I had got up to use the bathroom and didn't have the energy to wake her, so I sat on an old Queen Anne chair and watched her while I tried to decide how I'd tell her what I knew. I felt guilty sitting in the chair. It belonged to Natalie, my ex-wife, and there I was sitting in my wife's chair watching a naked woman sleep.

Fred woke me from my flashback to the night before by barking at the stick, daring me to pick it up. His tail began imitating a pendulum in anticipation of the chase. I absent-mindedly reached for his stick and found myself keeping time with his tail. His eyes followed the stick like it was a hypnotist's wand. Fred saw his chance and grabbed the stick. He was halfway up the road before I realized he had outfoxed me.

He was waiting for me where the trail going up the mountain intersected the road. Julie's camera had been placed a few yards away so it could capture anyone going up or coming down the trail. Like I'd suspected, the camera wasn't where she put it. I took out my cell phone and punched in Julie's mobile number.

"Hi, handsome," she said before I could open my mouth. "Miss me already?"

"I'm sorry. I must have the wrong number. The only handsome guy here is my dog and he ain't talking."

"Funny, Jake. Is the camera okay?"

"That's why I called you. It's gone. We can't find it anywhere. It's probably in some bull elk's antlers taking pictures of his female conquests."

Silence. The laughter was gone from her voice despite my sick humor.

"I'll have the techs turn on the GPS software. Do you mind sticking around? Once we get a signal I'll send you the parameters for you to track it with your cell phone."

Have I been out of the business that long? I didn't even know that was possible. "I hate to sound stupid, Julie, but how do I do that?"

Fred and I were sitting at our favorite spot on top of the hill watching the clouds drift by. It was the best place in the world I knew of where a man could escape, stop the clock, and think. The clouds were almost close enough to touch. Fred had laid his big head on my lap so I could scratch behind his ears. Waiting for Julie gave me plenty of time to reflect on who tried to blow up my motor home — with me in it.

Obviously, it was the poacher that Lonnie was blackmailing and it didn't take much imagination to see that he didn't want to, or couldn't, pay the blackmail. That cost Lonnie his life. Jonathan was the only one I could think of that had a motive. He needed money badly, and as Julie had told Bonnie, the Asian market for bear organs was extremely lucrative.

Jonathan's business and lifestyle were bleeding money, so I doubt if he had any extra to give Lonnie. He looked more and more like the poacher, but then I remembered the Corvette. Why would Lonnie sell his prize possession to Jonathan if he was blackmailing him? And what did Jonathan have to gain by destroying me and my motor home?

Was it me he was after? When framing me for the poaching didn't work, did he think a little gas leak and explosion would do the trick? If the motor home battery had been connected, I would be talking to Saint Peter after turning on the light switch. So why did he want me out of the way? I was working on that problem when my cell phone rang.

"Hi, sexy. Have I told you lately how hot you are?" I said without bothering to check my caller ID.

"Why thank you, Jake. I didn't know you liked me that much?" I swear I heard Bonnie giggling. Forget fifty shades of gray. I turned twice that many in red. "Sorry, Bonnie. I thought you were Julie."

"Oh, I knew that, Silly. This old broad don't miss a whole lot, you know. I kind of guessed you two were doing the hanky-panky last night when she didn't leave until this morning, but that ain't why I..." I missed her last words when call waiting cut her off.

"Let me call you back, Bon. I think its Julie." I flashed her off and answered the other line. This time I waited for the caller to talk.

"Jake?" It was indeed the voice of my angel.

"Hi, beautiful," I answered without being embarrassed. "Is the GPS chip turned on?"

"You won't be needing it. The techs say it won't respond." Then before I could ask why, she continued. "Besides, my boss overheard me asking you for help and freaked out."

"No need to explain, Julie. I worked for enough fortune five-hundred companies to guess what he said. Something on the order of me getting hurt and suing the State or maybe putting in a claim for payment as a contractor. Typical corporate BS. Or in the case of a government agency, worse than BS. More like Moose crap."

"Sorry. Why don't you come into town so I can make it up to you? I know this fantastic Italian restaurant on Thirty-Eighth Avenue and then you can do a little undercover work for me."

"What about your boss?"

She giggled before answering. "Not that kind of undercover, Goofy. Meet me at the restaurant at six. It's on the corner of Thirty-eighth and Teller. I should be out of here by then." It was becoming obvious that she was used to giving orders, and for once, I didn't mind taking them.

Her giggle reminded me of Bonnie. I went back to the other line. She was still waiting for me. "Sorry about that, Bon Bon. What's up?"

"Was that Julie?"

"Don't be jealous, my love." I answered in my best imitation of a gigolo. "I'm sure it's a passing infatuation."

"I told Margot what you told me."

"Oh, and what is that? I don't remember much after the first six-pack," I asked.

"Can you come off that mountain and talk to me, Jake. Margot is pissed again. I know I should have never said anything, but she is my sister you know."

"How'd you know we were up here?"

"A little birdie told me. Please, Jake? We need to talk."

Bonnie was waiting at my cabin when Fred and I came down from the mountain. She must have walked because her car was nowhere in sight and she was breathing like she just ran a marathon.

"Didn't your mother ever tell you cigarettes would stunt your growth," I said, pointing to the half-smoked cigarette in her hand.

She took a long drag then let the smoke out slowly. "One of life's few pleasures at my age, Sonny. "You should try it," she said and held out her cigarette in my direction.

That's when I noticed the funny smell and saw it was no store-bought cigarette. "Thanks, Bon, but I'll pass," I said and waved off her offer. "Why don't you come on in and tell me why Margot has you so upset?"

I held the door open, but she didn't budge. Her smile faded at the mention of her sister. She took one more drag from her homemade cigarette, then flicked it into the dirt.

"I should have never told her. I'm sorry, Jake. Really, I am." Bonnie looked like she was going to collapse right in front of me.

I reached out to steady her, and she grabbed me around the waist, burying her head into my chest. All I could think of is how terrible I must smell after climbing the mountain. I finally came to my senses and hugged her back.

Fred must have sensed my uneasiness, or at the least Bonnie's pain. He saw me looking at him and replied with a loud bark, then came over to us and pushed up against us.

"What's the matter, Freddie? Do you want your daddy?" Bonnie asked. She let go and reached down to pet Fred. She still wasn't smiling, but I could see Fred had softened the lines in her face somewhat.

"Margot wants to get a court order for your computer."

Now I was the one with a frown. "What on earth for?"

"It's the damn book," she answered, reaching behind her ear for a real cigarette. "She started yelling at me and babbling something about Charlie didn't deserve to have his father's reputation ruined because you couldn't leave well enough alone."

"Why don't you sit down, Bon, and light that thing? It looks like you need it. I'll get us a couple of beers and you can bring me up to date. Evidently there's something in your father's book I missed."

Bonnie stared at me for a moment. Her eyes were glazed over as though she was trying to process what I had said. Then she turned and sat down on one of my Adirondack chairs. Fred chose to stay with her while I hurried off for the beer that I had no intention of getting.

She was talking to Fred when I returned a few minutes later. "Fred must have drank the last one last night, Bon," I lied. "Hope you don't mind coffee instead. It will only be a minute. I've got it brewing now."

I scooted my rocker next to her. "Now why don't you tell me what got you so upset? I can't imagine it was the book. Margot would never have given it to me in the first place if that's what's bothering her."

She seemed to be coming around. Her face showed signs of deep concentration. "It was Charlie that got her going. Margot didn't realize she gave him the original. She had removed all the dirt from the copy."

I started to ask how Chuck got his chubby hands on the book, then realized Margot must have given him my copy. Then it dawned on me why she wanted my computer so badly.

"I had the original and not a copy?"

She nodded, lighting her cigarette.

"What's in there to get Chuck so riled up?" I asked.

"That part about the fragging. I didn't know you weren't supposed to see it when you told me about it. The sergeant who killed the lieutenant was Charlie's father."

I sat back in my rocker not knowing what to say. Luckily I didn't have to when I remembered the coffee. "Hold on, Bon," I said getting up. "My percolator is boiling over."

She followed me into the cabin and Fred followed her. "I told Margot I would get you to delete the file and promised to watch while you did it. Do you mind, Jake?"

"Not at all, come on in and I'll do it now. At least Margot saved me the time I would have spent searching war records for the sergeant who did the fragging. Chuck's father? Who would have guessed?"

Bonnie seemed satisfied after I deleted her father's book from my computer. I even went so far as making a show of giving her a backup CD and several pages of a printout I had been working with, but she wasn't completely computer illiterate; she asked, then watched, as I emptied my computer's wastebasket. I didn't mention how easy it would be for me to restore the file once she left. I made sure she had several cups of coffee before I asked her to watch Fred while I went into town to have dinner with Julie.

Once she left with my buddy, I showered, shaved and dusted off a pair of pants and dress shirt I hadn't worn since my last job interview. When I got to the tie, I noticed a crease made by the hanger it had been hanging on the last six months and decided to ditch the whole outfit. Eventually I settled for a casual pair of khakis, sport shirt with a collar, and a comfortable pair of hiking boots.

Talk about a fish out of water. The restaurant no longer resembled the family oriented eatery I remembered. The checkered tablecloths and plastic ware had been replaced by fine linen and gold-trimmed china. I half expected the maître d' to offer me a coat and tie when I explained I didn't have reservations and was looking for Julie. Even the waiter who led me to Julie's table was dressed better than me. I soon forgot about my attire when I saw her sitting at a table set away in a little alcove by itself. She was stunning. Until now I had only seen her dressed in a uniform with her hair sticking out the back of a cap in a ponytail. She must have spent hours getting the curls that flowed like braids over her shoulders. She was studying a menu and quickly put away her reading glasses when she saw me approaching.

"Aren't you a handsome devil," she said.

"Sorry I'm late. My chauffeur couldn't find the keys to my Rolls so I had to borrow his car and the parking valet didn't recognize me when I pulled up. Can you believe they made me park the car myself?" I asked while taking a seat across from her.

Julie laughed at my remark, but it didn't seem to faze our waiter. "Our special tonight is a tender veal-Parmesan covered in a spicy-tomato sauce and served on a bed of vermicelli," he said, in a phony Italian accent while handing me a menu. "And if I may suggest the Montepulciano. You will find the full-bodied flavor a perfect complement to the hand-chosen herbs and spices our chef uses in all our pastas."

Julie raised her glass in a toast. "You should try this wine, Jake. They import it all the way from California," she said, suppressing a giggle.

"Can I get a bottle of beer? Nothing fancy, Bud or Coors will do," I said, still trying to get the waiter to show some emotion. "Oh, and I don't need a glass."

Julie held her hand to her face. I could see by the lines in her forehead that she was trying not to laugh.

"Do you think I'm over dressed?" I asked after the waiter left. "Maybe that's why he wouldn't smile."

"You made me smile, Jake," she said, taking a sip of wine. The dim light from a nearby lamp caught the crystal perfectly, playing across her beautiful face. "You have no idea how I needed that after the day I've had."

"Your boss?" I asked.

Her smile turned to a frown. "What a prick. You'd think he'd be happy I tried to recruit you. He's always harping about the budget. I find some free labor and all he can do is recite the riot act about you getting hurt on the job and suing us."

"Forget about him, Julie. Tell me how to track down that camera. What he doesn't know won't hurt him."

She started to say something else, then stopped short and looked beyond me. Our waiter was back and just in time. I really needed my beer.

"Have you decided?" he asked, not bothering with the accent.

I twisted off the cap on the bottle he had placed on the table without opening it. I waited for Julie to go first while I took a long swallow. Somehow I knew she would prefer to order for herself. She ordered the special.

"I'll have the same," I said when it was my turn.

"You're a sweetheart, Jake," she said after our waiter left. "But I've worked too hard and given up too much to get where I am. I can't jeopardize it all just to save the department a few dollars."

Her response almost didn't register. I had been watching her talk and was nearly hypnotized by the way her lips turned up at the corner when she spoke.

"Hello. Earth to Jake. Did you hear anything I said?"

"Sorry. I was counting freckles." Her hand went to her face self-consciously and I swear she blushed, although it was hard to tell with her complexion.

"Do you think it's possible to fall in love at first sight?"

"With freckles?" she asked.

"Yes, freckles and all. Now if you don't answer pretty soon, I'm going to be the one who's embarrassed."

Suddenly the room seemed to go quiet and the temperature drop twenty degrees. None of it actually happened, but it sure felt that way. I knew her answer from the sadness in her eyes.

"I can't do this to you, Jake. I should have told you instead of making up that stupid excuse of being on a date."

"You didn't have a date?" It sounded stupid the minute I said it. I should have asked what she meant, but was too surprised about her confession.

"No. I was too tired," she answered. The woman who could stare down a raging bull wouldn't look at me. "I didn't think it would ever come to this."

A thousand thoughts went through my mind trying to guess what she was talking about. This time I kept my mouth shut and just waited until she looked up from the table into my eyes. She had real tears pouring down her cheeks.

"I'm dying, Jake. It was in remission for two years, but the cancer has come back."

I reached across the table and took her hands in mine. "It doesn't change how I feel about you, Julie. I'll help you beat it. I'll sell my house or even my soul if that's what it takes to get you well again."

"Damn. Why did you have to go and fall in love with me?"

I took the back road past Red Rocks and through Morrison so I could lick my wounds. I had plenty of time to think on the way home. Julie had regained her composure after a short trip to the ladies' room and told me the rest of the story. She had been diagnosed with Hodgkin's Lymphoma six years ago. She had already outlived the average patient and her doctors thought she had beat it, but the fevers and fatigue were back. She was confident she could recover, but like before, it would take serious chemotherapy, which she didn't want me to see her go through.

Julie wanted to tell me more, but our annoying waiter interrupted with our meals and she changed the subject after he left. She didn't want to talk about it anymore and made small-talk all through dinner. She even insisted on picking up the tab before we left, claiming she could write it off. In the end, I became nothing more than a business expense since she never once said she loved me too.

The town of Kittredge was a blur in my mirror when I gave Bonnie a call.

"Wow, Jake. Do you have ESP or is my place wired? I was just talking about you."

"Neither, Bon Bon, but I do need a drink and a friendly face to talk to. I'm on my way home. I should be there in a few minutes to get Fred. How about I stop by the liquor store and pick up some beer?"

"I've got a better idea, Dear. Meet us at Little Bear. I'll drop Fred off at your place and come down to meet you."

"Consider it a date, Sunshine. I'll see you in fifteen minutes." The 'us' didn't register until after I hung up.

Bonnie couldn't have picked a worse place for a quiet drink. The Little Bear was packed when I got there. I passed the place three times trying to find a parking space. The lot across the street was out of the question since they had raised their prices for the coming tourist season. I finally found a spot up the road by the lake and walked back to the bar. I found Bonnie sitting at a far table talking to an overweight man whose back was to me. I knew who it was even without the oxygen tank next to him.

"It's okay, Jake, he won't bite." Bonnie was beaming. "Sit down, Charlie would like to buy you a beer. Wouldn't you Chuck?"

I heard him mumble something when I took the seat at the end of the table. It was a small rectangle of a table with one end up against the wall, leaving only enough room for three chairs. My chair was sticking out in what little room passed as an aisle between it and the crowded table next to us.

"What do I owe the pleasure to, Charlie? You have another restraining order you wanted to deliver personally?"

Chuck's expression didn't change. I suppose after selling cars for forty years, his phony smile couldn't have been more set in place if it had been chiseled on his face.

"Shelia is willing to drop her suit if you will sign a little document for us. I thought it'd be better to meet you in person; you know, man to man, and keep the DA out of it."

"The DA? What the hell does the district attorney have to do with anything? When did this become a criminal case?"

Bonnie reached over and held my hand to the table. "Please, Jake. He's only trying to do what's best for everyone." Her touch had its intended effect. I unclenched my fist and felt my blood pressure drop several points.

The conversation at the table next to us had gone silent. Bonnie must have noticed too. She turned in their direction and delicately showed them her middle finger. "Hear him out, Jake, he's trying to apologize," she said after our neighbors went back to whatever they had been discussing.

"It's not an apology!" Chuck said with a voice louder than usual. His chiseled face was starting to erode with streaks of red.

"Sorry," Bonnie replied. "Guess I had a little too much to drink again."

Chuck checked on the table next to us then shifted his large mass back to face me and pushed a formal looking document toward me. "Here's the deal, Jake. Lonnie left Shelia some insurance. It had a double indemnity clause. I don't suppose you know what that means..."

I cut him off, "I'm not an idiot, Chuck. It pays double if he dies in an accident."

"Or negligent homicide," he continued. "The insurance company says he died of heart failure and is fighting payment. My lawyers say if they can prove he died because of your negligence, they can beat the insurance company. So sign this affidavit saying you screwed up, or my friends down at the courthouse will be charging you for manslaughter. Personally, I'd rather see you spend the next twenty years in jail, but Bonnie called in a favor to save your sorry ass."

Once more the people at the next table quit talking and were all ears. Bonnie was getting ready to flip them off again when a guy with a long-gray ponytail and leather vest came over and put his hand on my shoulder.

"Don't do it, Bud," he said.

The whole bar went silent. Except for Johnny Paycheck telling his boss where to put his job, you could hear a mouse fart. Scenes from a bad biker movie ran through my head. *Should I hit the guy or run?* I didn't have to decide. Before I could act he reached into his back pocket and brought out a wallet tied to a chain on his belt.

"I work for a law firm in Littleton during the week. From what I've heard so far, it sounds like you need a lawyer."

Then a heavyset woman with streaks of gray grabbed my new friend by the arm. "Bobby, we need to go."

Bobby ignored her and turned to Chuck. "You should know better, Mister Randolph. Those kinds of tactics might work in your showroom, but you're treading on coercion."

Bobby's girlfriend, or whoever she was, kept pulling him away. "Come on, Bobby, my mom ain't gonna watch the kids all night."

"Call me before you sign anything, Pal," he said while his woman dragged him away. It wasn't long before their friends got up and left too.

I took a slow, drawn-out look at the card the lawyer had given me. People at the other tables went back to their own little dramas or whatever they were discussing before we had taken center stage.

"Nice try, Chuck," I said, looking up once I felt it was time. "If all this were over a car you were trying to sell me, I'd tell you to take your deal and shove it, just like the song. But forcing me to admit I'm guilty of something I didn't do is not another car deal. So here's my deal, and I don't give a rat's ass if you like it or not. There's negligence alright, but not because of me. I've got proof that Lonnie's death was no accident. I'm going to talk to this lawyer tomorrow and press a suit of my own for your constant harassment, intimidation, and collusion."

Both Chuck and Bonnie looked at me with their mouths open. I didn't wait for a response. I threw a ten dollar bill on the table and walked out. I had plenty of time to consider my words on the walk to my Jeep. I didn't know if intimidation and collusion were legal terms or not, but they sure sounded good at the time.

I expected to hear from Bonnie on my way home asking what proof I had that Lonnie's death was not an accident. I even stopped off at the liquor store between the church and Safeway, giving her time to call before I'd lose my cell signal going up the canyon. At least that was the excuse I gave myself. Truth be told, I really needed a beer.

Bonnie's call never came, so I decided to drive by her place on the way home. I had the bright idea to apologize by sharing my twelve-pack. Her place wasn't that far out of the way of my normal route. We both lived on Columbine Circle, but I usually didn't pass her house because she was on the left fork, which took longer than going the other way. Either way worked, so tonight I turned left instead of right. She must not have come home yet. Her car wasn't in the drive and the place was completely dark. However, I could see up the hill to my cabin. Someone was up there who wasn't supposed to be. Unless Fred had learned to turn on my lantern by himself, I had another intruder.

Chapter 11

Not wanting to alert whoever was in my cabin, I drove past Bonnie's until I was out of sight then parked my Jeep. From there I walked back to her house and climbed the path between our two houses. The intruder could have a weapon, so I needed to surprise whoever it was. My defense was a twelve-pack of beer and an aspen stick I found on the trek up the hill.

My cabin is built on a slope with a walkout basement. I stopped to catch my breath when I reached the lower level. I was breathing in and out faster than an air compressor. Once I could hear above the noise of my lungs, I heard someone talking. *Did this guy like to talk to himself, or was there more than one intruder?*

My weapons were no match for a pair of burglars. I decided to sneak around to my motor home where I could at least get a large knife to defend myself. I barely made it to the coach's door when I was blinded by a powerful beam of light coming from my cabin.

"Whoever is sneaking around out there, I've got a gun and a guard dog."

"It's me, Bonnie. Jake," I answered, recognizing her voice. "You nearly gave me a heart attack."

"Gave you a heart attack? What about me and Fred?" She no sooner said his name than I heard him bark and come running to me.

Fred was so happy to see me, he nearly knocked me over. He could almost put his paws on my shoulders when he stood on his hind legs. I grabbed his head between my hands and bent down to hug him the best I could.

"Did you miss your dad, old Boy?"

"I should have known it was you." Bonnie had followed Fred over to the motor home. "He's been wagging his tail ever since you came snooping around down below. What the hell was that all about anyway?"

Fred gave up trying to wash my face and sat down by my feet. I petted him one more time, then looked over at my neighbor. "I thought someone broke in. Let's go back inside. I'll tell you all about it over a beer."

Bonnie and I nearly finished off the twelve-pack in no time with a little help from Fred. I poured a few ounces in a bowl, but it wasn't the same as pouring it on the cedar deck boards. The beer didn't produce the bubbles he loved to bite. Somewhere between the third and fourth beers I told her about my breakup with Julie.

"She has cancer?"

"Hodgkin's," I said then opened another beer for both of us.

She finished the beer she had been drinking and took a new one. "Why didn't you just hug her and kiss her and tell her it's okay? Girls like that sort of thing, you know."

"I tried, Bon. Believe me, I really tried."

Bonnie took a deep drink, then looked at me with tears in her eyes. "You should've kissed her anyway."

We were sitting at my table, so I reached for a paper towel from a roll I had on my kitchen counter and handed it to her. "Okay. I told you my story, now it's your turn.

After wiping her face, she told me how Chuck had fooled her into the meeting at Little Bear. She swore she had no knowledge of the affidavit. She truly believed he wanted to apologize.

She had taken her Bronco to his dealership for servicing earlier. Margot picked her up so they could go shopping at the mall while her car was being worked on. Chuck was waiting for her when she returned to pick it up. He said they had to keep the car overnight and offered to give her a ride home. That was when he tricked her into the meeting at Little Bear.

I had a hard time trying to decide whose side she was on. She kept quizzing me about the evidence I said could prove Lonnie's death was not my fault. I think it was after beer number five or six that I let it slip about the propane tank.

Fred let me sleep in the next morning. It was nearly noon when Bonnie called to ask me if I could give her a ride into town. Chuck wasn't so eager to drive back up the mountain now that he got what he wanted from her. He did say he would have someone bring her the

Bronco, but it might be a day or two before his service manager could schedule it.

"No hurry, Jake. I've got some things to do before we go. Is this afternoon okay with you?" she asked.

Fred woke and begged to be let out.

"No problem, Bon. Fred wants out, so I think I take him for a hike. Call when you're ready."

After having second thoughts about the hike, I left the door open so he could come back in on his own. I doubt if his hangover came close to the way I was feeling. I have no idea how much alcohol a dog can tolerate, but it had to be more than a few laps of the tongue. His bowl was barely touched. That became apparent when I tripped over it and spilled it on the floor.

Fred was back in time to hear a few choice cuss words. Lucky for me, I chose a dog for a pet instead of a parrot. The spill would soak into my floors by the time I fetched the mop from the storage shed next to my motor home. I had left it there after cleaning up from the first break-in. I decided to do the next best thing and tried to get Fred to clean up for me.

"Come and get your breakfast, Fred," He didn't move from the doorway. "I'm sorry, Freddie. I didn't mean to swear at you." He still didn't budge, so I went into the kitchen and got a hot dog out of my cooler. I broke it into several small pieces and spread them in the puddle.

Robovac sprang into action and devoured the hot dog, then lapped up the rest of the mess. It soon became evident that my four-legged vacuum cleaner was making the mess worse. Now, instead of a puddle of beer, I had dog spit on my floor. It was time to fetch the mop.

That's when I discovered any hope of beating Chuck's vendetta to hang me was gone. Besides the mop and a few garden tools, I had also put Jonathan's propane bottle in the shed. I knew before I opened the door that the tank would be gone. The latch on my storage shed had been pried from the door with the lock still intact. Whoever broke in found it much easier to rip it off the door than to break the lock.

"What the f..," I said when I confirmed its absence. This time I caught myself before finishing the cuss word. "Why would your aunt Bonnie steal our tank?" Fred had followed me to the shed, presumably looking for more hotdogs.

Fred answered with a bark. He was giving me his let's play look. He barked again, then ran up the road to where the game camera had been.

I closed the shed's door the best I could, and started for my cabin. I was in no mood to play fetch. Someone stole the only hope I had to beat Shelia's lawsuit. The last thing I wanted to do was play with sticks.

Why would Bonnie steal the tank? I asked myself over and over. At least an hour had passed since the discovery of the break-in. I was sitting on the porch in the rocker Bonnie had given me, racking my brain for answers. I even asked Fred twice, but all he would do is run back up the road each time I asked. I didn't want to play so I quit asking him and resorted to talking to myself.

It was pretty obvious I had implied someone used the tank to commit murder. I didn't want to confront Bonnie with the theft. Maybe it wasn't her and it would only hurt her feelings. Besides, what motive could she have to possibly kill Lonnie? No, it had to be Charlie Randolph. Unless it was someone at the Little Bear who overheard me say the explosion wasn't an accident, but that didn't make sense either. What were the odds a perfect stranger killed Lonnie?

All this deductive reasoning brought me back to Charlie as the murderer, but he could never have ripped the lock off my shed. Not in his physical condition. Of course, he could have sent someone to do his dirty work. Then there was also the possibility Bonnie might have called Margot and she in turn called Jonathan to tell him I had his tank. After all it was Jonathan's tank, but why would he come up here in the middle of the night and steal it? All he had to do was knock on my door and demand it back or worse yet, send the law to get it.

Fred barked again, and pointed back up the road. Golden retrievers were never bred to point out game, but Fred did a pretty good imitation of an Irish Setter. Then the synapses finally connected. Who said beer will fry a dog's brain? It seemed to be doing wonders for Fred.

"Damn, Fred. You've got to be the smartest dog since Lassie." I finally realized what my dog knew all along. The tank wasn't taken last night. The intruder who tried to blow up my motor home must have taken it. He wasn't after me at all. It was a subterfuge to hide the theft of the propane tank.

However smart my dog was, he still couldn't tell me how I was going to get the tank back so I could prove Lonnie's accident wasn't my fault.

"So what now, Genius?" I didn't really expect Fred to answer. It was a habit I had cultivated to help me think. "Got any more ideas? Like how to track down that tank?"

Fred sat looking at me, taking it all in. "Exactly what I was thinking," I said to him. "Julie said the camera had a GPS chip just like my cell phone. Let's see if we can't hack into it and track it down. Whoever stole Julie's camera did so because they thought it might have taken a picture of their getaway vehicle, and I'll bet you dollars to your slimy sticks that it's the same person who killed Lonnie." Fred didn't really tell me all this, vocally or through telepathy, but he would have if he could.

We went back to my cabin and booted up my laptop. There was a good chance the camera took more than one picture of the getaway vehicle. The one that got loaded to the server wasn't much help, but what if there were more?

Within an hour I found an app for my smart phone that would pinpoint the GPS chip within a few feet, but it required the chip's IP address. So I went to a site that specializes in shady software and found another app that would display the IP addresses of any device broadcasting within a few hundred yards. There was a good chance that Julie's cameras would be within a few digits of one another. If this spy app could tell me the addresses of her other cameras, I should be able to figure out the address of the missing one. With luck, I will find the camera and get the pictures of my intruder from the camera's SIM card.

"Let's go back up the hill, Freddie. We've got some snooping to do." I said to my bored sidekick. The excitement of the internet search had put him to sleep at my feet.

I didn't need to ask Fred twice. He was up and out the door before I could finish loading the spy app. I caught up with him at the intersection of the road and our mountain trail. He took off again, running to where the missing camera had been and picked up something before running back to me.

Fred wouldn't last a day as a bird dog. He loved to retrieve, but never learned that a retriever was supposed to drop the fowl at his owner's feet. Fred wanted me to grab it and play tug of war. I could see now that Fred's prize was the cable Julie used to attach her camera to a tree. I ignored Fred and walked over to where he found the cable. He followed me like a shadow, with the cable between his teeth.

I let my eyes drift to Fred's cable. I could see it had not been a clean cut. The cable was made with dozens of steel wires wound together, and they were all frayed and uneven. It must have been some kind of ax, or dull blade, used to cut the cable.

"Guess we won't be asking for an APB on Bullwinkle, Freddie. If it was an elk, he's toothless now. Look at this tree. They nearly chopped it down trying to cut through that cable."

Whoever took the camera must not have planned on stealing it. I doubt if he even knew it was here until he saw the flash. An image of surprise on his face flashed in my head. I wondered how long it took him to realize it was a game camera and not lightning or some other flash that had just snapped his picture leaving a crime scene.

I reached for the cable. Fred took my action as a sign that the game was on. He tightened his grip and backed up a few feet. He was daring me to try and take it from him. "Damn it, Fred. Give me the friggin cable." It was all he needed to take off up the trail.

I chased after him until we reached the part of the trail close to where the bear had been dissected. Fred smelled death in the air. He dropped the cable and went straight to the scene of the crime. The bear was long gone after being removed by Julie's crew, but I could see Julie's second camera. She had installed it after finding the bear carcass, so I turned on my phone and started the IP sniffing app. Within a few minutes I had an address and the cable. When Fred saw me pick it up, he went into receiving mode waiting for me to throw it. "Forget it, Freddie. This is evidence and I'm sure Julie won't appreciate dog spittle contaminating it. Now shall we get back to work?"

Although I knew where the third camera was hidden, I used it to test my theory. After switching to the locator app on my smart phone, I tried an IP address one greater than the bear camera. Sure enough, there it was on the map. Then I tried an IP address that was one less than the bear camera. The app found it almost immediately. The location was on West Colfax. I switched to satellite view and zoomed in.

"What the..." I said out loud. Fred turned his head as if to hear me better. He had been sitting and watching me. "The camera is in the middle of Randolph Motors' parking lot. Why am I not surprised?"

I was still staring at the satellite image when my phone started ringing. I nearly dropped it into the jaws of my wide receiver. "Bonnie, I was just thinking of you." I didn't mention that my shed had been ransacked and the propane tank missing was why I was thinking of her.

"Then you didn't forget you promised to give me a ride?" she asked.

"Not at all. Fred and I were out for a hike and lost track of time. Are you ready to go into town? We can be at your place in fifteen minutes."

"Thank you, Jake. You don't need to rush. The service manager said he would leave my keys in the showroom if I don't get there before six. As long as I pick it up before they close is fine."

I didn't tell her how happy I was to give her a ride to Randolph Motors. It was the perfect cover for me to check out the exact spot where the GPS said I'd find the missing camera. The satellite image I saw was several weeks, if not months, out of date, which made visual identification impossible. I assumed it was in a vehicle, but which one was impossible to tell from the map image.

Randolph Motors had been in the same location for over sixty years. It was a landmark of sorts. Just like thousands before me, I found it without any help from my GPS, but landmark or not, Bonnie had my smart phone in her lap with the locator app turned on.

"Isn't that your girlfriend, Jake?" She asked when I drove into the parking lot. She had spotted Julie at the side of the service building, talking to a couple cops by the dumpsters. I could see a DOW agent standing in one of them holding what looked like a game camera.

"Funny, Bon," I answered while looking for a parking place. I didn't remind her that Julie had dumped me less than twenty-four hours ago. I chose a parking spot next to a familiar looking truck. We were about as close as we could get to the action without drawing attention to ourselves.

"I think they beat us to it," Bonnie said, handing me my phone. "That looks like the camera you described."

We watched as the DOW agent climbed out of the dumpster with the camera in hand. Julie must have been in charge. Her partner handed her the camera before he hit the ground. I could see it was in pieces.

Julie handed the security case back to her partner, who was now on the ground, and opened the back of the camera. I didn't have to be a lip reader to see what she said. Her language didn't seem to offend her partner; however, all the cops stopped talking and looked at her. She must have sensed their stares. She spotted us when she looked up from the camera to say something. She handed the camera back to her partner and came over to my Jeep. Fred recognized her and barked out a hello.

"What are you doing here, Freddie?" she asked when she reached over to pet him on the head. He had half his body out the rear window by now. Then she stooped down to look at me.

Her expression was all business. Not even a carnival fortune teller could have guessed we had been lovers. I knew better than to tell her how much I missed her, and wanted her back. It would be like throwing water on a grease fire.

"Bonnie needed a ride," I answered for Fred. She left her car for service yesterday. What's going on anyway? I didn't know you were into dumpster diving?"

I thought I saw her beautiful green eyes turn a shade lighter. "For a minute there, I thought you figured out a way to track the camera. I know you're smart, but not that smart. Are you?"

"Is that what was in the dumpster?" I asked, trying my best to act surprised.

She didn't answer right away. She just stared into my eyes like she was able to read my thoughts. Finally, she broke the trance and spoke. "Call me later. We need to talk." Then she turned and walked away.

I was still watching her ponytail swing back and forth, and feeling depressed when Bonnie woke me from my self-pity. "I think she's on to us, Jake," she said.

I put the Jeep in gear and drove over to the service area where a familiar looking face came to greet us.

"Long time no see, Amigo. You come to trade in the old tin-can?"

"Mario?" I asked. I didn't recognize him at first in clean clothes and a tie.

"Yeah. My cousin works here as the service manager and put in a word for me," he said, grabbing my door jamb so I'd have to run him over if I wanted to leave." It don't pay much, but the checks don't bounce."

His phony smile told me he would make a great car salesman. "Well, Mario. I'll be sure to see you first if I ever win the lotto." Bonnie had already left so I started my Jeep hoping he'd let go.

He must have realized he was wasting his time trying to sell me a car and removed his hand from my Jeep, but not before sticking a card in my face. "I'll be waiting, Amigo," he said and left.

Fred rode shotgun on the way home. When he wasn't sticking his head out the window to bite the wind, he would lay it on my lap so I could rub his ears. I was still thinking about why I had to ruin a perfectly good sex life by falling in love when we turned off I-70 onto Evergreen Parkway and Fred spotted McDonald's. He barked once, then looked at me with his sad-puppy eyes.

"Okay, Boy, as long as you don't tell Julie." I realized too late that there was a fat chance of that.

I pulled into the drive-up lane behind a familiar looking truck. It had camouflage paint and bumper stickers plastered on the tailgate. They included stickers supporting the NRA, chewing tobacco and one that read 'I Got High in Colorado', and right under that was one with an 'I' a heart and a picture of a marijuana leaf. I had seen dozens of stickers like these, except for the references to marijuana, on pickup trucks in Missouri last summer, but only one recently; that was at Bonnie's barbeque. This truck wasn't Alec's, and the driver wasn't him, but it was all I needed to put the pieces together.

Fred gulped down his McDouble in record time. We had stopped at a picnic area in Bergen Park to make my call and eat our burgers. While waiting for Bonnie to pick up, I gave Fred my hamburger. She answered before he could finish it.

"What's the matter, Jake? Did you break down or are you just lonesome?"

I couldn't think of a cute comeback and I really wasn't in the mood to give one. "Are you home yet, Bon?"

"Almost. I'm crossing our little bridge now. Is something wrong? You sound upset."

I started to say I knew why the barbeque blew up, then had second thoughts. I needed more time to think how I was going to tell her Alec was making meth. "We need to talk about Alec and that propane tank, Bon. Can I stop by?"

Silence. Then I heard fear in her voice. "Are you going to tell the police, Jake?"

"Police? Why would I do that?"

More silence. This time the pause was much shorter. "Because if you don't, you will be an accessory. I can't do that to you, Jake."

"Let's not talk about this over the phone. You never know who's listening. I'll be there in twenty minutes." I hung up before she could say anymore.

It actually took me closer to an hour. I got caught up in a traffic jam just before the Safeway shopping center. Someone had run into the back of a septic-pumping truck. The smell was so bad, I decided to pull off and make a pit stop at the liquor store. They had Canadian Club on sale, so I bought a pint for Bonnie and a twelve pack of Keystone for me and Fred. It took most of my cash, but I figured it might help her open up about Alec. It appeared to be working.

"I can be dense sometimes, Bon Bon. I should have seen it was Alec long ago," I said while mixing her a glass of CC and coke. She had invited me and Fred into her kitchen. She was sitting at the table while I fumbled around by the sink. "It wasn't until I realized the tank was filled with anhydrous ammonia that I put two and two together."

She had her head in her hands and seemed depressed until I mentioned her nephew. "You think Alec killed Lonnie?" she asked.

I handed her the drink and paused before getting my beer from her refrigerator where I had put it to keep cold. "Who said anything about Lonnie? I'm talking about meth."

"Meth?"

"Yeah, I think I saw it in a movie, or maybe I read it somewhere. It doesn't matter. What matters is the tank wasn't filled with propane. Alec filled it with anhydrous ammonia to make meth. At first I thought Alec had accidentally switched the tanks with your grill, but that theory evaporated with the smell of the septic truck. Ammonia stinks a lot worse than propane and the barbeque tank didn't have a smell."

She looked confused. "Septic truck?" she asked. "What are you talking about, Jake?"

I joined her and Fred at the table, "At first I thought that's why it was leaking. Anhydrous ammonia is very corrosive and can't be stored in regular propane tanks without leaking after a while. Then when we ran into a traffic jam involving a septic truck, I realized your tank didn't smell. I must have taken the wrong tank from Jon's roofing yard. I thought it was the one from your barbeque because of a cut hose. Evidently someone didn't have a wrench to unscrew the regulator and just cut the hose."

Bonnie finished half her drink while I explained how meth is made using ammonia. Somewhere toward the end of my lecture, she needed a smoke so we moved out to her porch.

"So it was Alec who broke into your shed? He wanted his tank back, didn't he?" she asked before taking a long drag on her cigarette.

"Exactly what I thought," I answered.

"What about the camera, Jake? What if they see Alec's truck in those pictures? It's bound to come out sooner or later."

I moved my chair away from her smoke, pretending to get a better view of Fred. He was more interested in chasing Chatter the squirrel than listening to our conversation. "There won't be any pictures. Alec, or whoever took the camera, was smart enough to remove the memory card. That was the first thing I noticed when Julie showed us the camera."

"I'm sorry, Jake. I should quit these nasty things, but they help calm me at times like this," she said while dropping the stub in one of my empty beer cans. "Does Julie know about the meth?"

For a person who had put away close to a pint of whiskey, I couldn't fathom why she wasn't already calm, but let it go. "Not unless she figured it out herself. My lips are sealed."

She poured the rest of her Canadian Club into her glass, taking it straight this time. "I've got to fix myself something to eat before my blood-sugar goes haywire. Would you and Fred like to stay for dinner?"

"No, but thanks anyway. We stopped at McDonald's on the way back." I didn't mention that Fred ate both our hamburgers. "By the way, Bon. Does Alec work for Chuck?"

She stopped short of entering her house. She stood with one hand on the doorknob and turned to face me. "Not that I've heard. Why do you ask? Oh, I see where this is going. It's because of the camera, isn't it? You think Alec threw it in Chuck's dumpster."

"You see right through me, Bon."

"I'm sorry we dragged you into this, Jake. Families should keep their dirty laundry to themselves," she said and went inside, closing the door behind her.

Bonnie didn't give me a chance to tell her about my conversation with Linda Grabowski and my discovery of the Corvette. She hadn't exactly slammed the door in my face, but somehow I was left feeling like a door-to-door vacuum salesman. I was still thinking about her while preparing dinner for Fred and myself.

Back when I still had dependable electricity, dinner would have been a TV dinner. Now we had to eat whatever canned food I could scrounge from the cupboards and heat it over my camp stove. Fred didn't care. He would eat anything as long as it wasn't dog food. Tonight it was raviolis and sardines in mustard sauce. I ate half the can of raviolis and then decided against the sardines. Fred gobbled down the leftovers like it was his last meal while I punched in Julie's number on my phone. I quickly changed my mind and pushed the off button.

I really wanted to call her. Really, I did, but I couldn't. As much as I needed to ask her if she knew how the camera found its way into Chuck's dumpster, my pride wouldn't let me. She made it clear that she wasn't interested in me the way I was her. If she wanted to talk, she was going to have to call me first.

Chapter 12

I had told myself before I went to bed that I was through playing detective and needed to get back to finding some gainful employment. Living off the grid might be romantic to some but it was the pits and although my ex wife didn't bug me for money, my creditors did. Natalie had agreed to take a second on the cabin when we divorced. The market had been down and I really didn't want to sell, so she agreed to let me pay her half of what it was worth in one hundred-twenty payments. I was two months behind on both of the mortgages. Still, my plan to get up early to look for work failed. Fred woke me instead with his barking. It wasn't his "let me out to do my business" bark. We had company.

I managed to pull on some pants and reach the front door at the same time our visitor started knocking. "What's up, Tommy? Why aren't you in school today? Are you playing hooky?" I asked after opening the door. He was my neighbor's son from down by the creek.

"Sort of, Mister Martin. I missed the bus and dad didn't have the gas to drive me," he answered while studying my bare feet. "I was wondering if you could help out our troop. If I can sell enough magazine subscriptions, I can win a new bike too."

Ordinarily I would make some lame excuse and send the kid packing. It's not that I'm related to the Grinch like my wife says. It's that the families on Upper Bear Creek have more weekly disposable income than I make all year. They don't send their kids out soliciting for good causes, they simply write a check. But Bonnie had told me about the Hatches. Tommy's mother committed suicide when she was diagnosed with stage four breast cancer; then a month after the funeral, the father's company filed for bankruptcy. They were living on unemployment until the insurance company paid on the mother's life insurance. That had been six months ago and the father was still trying to collect.

Fred wasted no time trying to get Tommy to play. He picked up a nearby stick and tried to put it in his hand. They had played this game many times when I took Fred for walks down by Bear Creek, but Tommy wasn't in the mood today and ignored him.

"Sure, Tommy, wait here while I get my wallet."

Tommy smiled and took Fred's stick. "Thank you, Mister Martin. Thanks a lot."

My cabin is small; I wasn't gone more than two minutes. Tommy and Fred were in a tug a war. He gave up and ran up to the porch when he saw me. "I'm a little short on cash, Tommy. Can you take a check?"

"Uh huh. Here's the list of magazines. Just pick the one you want and write the check for that amount."

I filled out the check without picking a magazine, and scribbled my name. "You pick something for me,

Tommy, I don't have the time right now. Have your dad fill out who you want the check made out to.

"Thanks, Mister Martin," he said and looked over the check like he'd never seen one before. "Wow, Mister Martin. Thanks. Thanks a lot."

I was the one smiling after he left, and I didn't lie about not having time to chit-chat. I needed to get to the bank and cover the two-hundred dollar check with a cash withdrawal from my credit card.

My cell started ringing before I could stop Fred from chasing after Tommy. "Jake, Alec is missing." Bonnie was frantic. It even sounded like she was crying.

"Missing?"

"Margot called this morning. He took off right after I told her about that tank. Nobody's heard or seen him since. It's not like Alec to stay out all night. Not without calling. I think he must have had an accident or something."

I wasn't surprised she had called Margot. I felt a bit betrayed, then got over it. Blood is thicker than CC and coke. "I'm sure he's okay, Bon Bon. He probably had a few too many and is sleeping it off at a friend's somewhere. What can I do to help?"

"We were wondering if you could track Alec's phone with that trick you used to find the camera."

"We?" I asked. "You told Margot. I could get in a lot of trouble, Bonnie. God, I hope she hasn't told Chuck.

I'm sure he would find a way to have me arrested for unlawful snooping or something."

She didn't answer right away, so I knew Margot must have told Chuck. "I'm sorry, Jake, but if you can help us I'm sure Margot will get him off your back. Please? Please see if you can track him?"

"It's not that easy, Bonnie. The app I downloaded won't track a phone that hasn't had the same app loaded on it, but I think there is a way to track any phone with a GPS chip just the same. I know the NSA has been spying on us that way, so maybe I can find something on the internet."

"Oh, thank you, Jake. Bring your laptop and smart phone. You can find that app while I whip up some breakfast for you and Fred. Then we can go looking for Alec's phone like we did that camera yesterday." She sounded like a teenager gossiping with her best friend. Worry over Alec had been usurped with the excitement of another adventure.

Two hours later the three of us were in my Wagoneer and headed for Idaho Springs taking the back road past Echo Lake. I made the two-hundred dollar deposit to cover Tommy's check over the phone and then found a computer program that could track any phone with a GPS. It wasn't free, but Bonnie had no problem using her credit card to pay for it. Unfortunately, all we had was the GPS coordinates and an aerial map of Alec's cell phone location. The program claimed the phone hadn't moved in over ten hours and was located in the hills above Idaho Springs. I put the coordinates into my smart phone, hoping it would lead us to Alec.

I knew the area well. It was an old mining district that I used to hike and camp when I was younger. It was inaccessible by anything other than four-wheel drive or a mule. The area was full of abandoned mine shafts that went hundreds of feet straight down. Most of them had once been covered with tall sheds containing cages that were lowered and raised with giant winches. That equipment had been sold off long ago for scrap and the sheds burned to the ground. Now there was nothing left but open pits that would put fear in Dante himself.

We decided to take my Jeep instead of her Bronco because my Wagoneer had the old Quadatrac drive-train with true four-wheel drive; unlike her Bronco where only one wheel per axel works, my Jeep used all four wheels. The area hadn't changed a lot since my youth. I had read once where it was nearly impossible to get a clear title to property in the region because of overlapping mining claims. The land had never really been developed for housing, and no new roads built in years. It was mining country where miners would stake a claim and dig their exploratory holes. There wasn't a square inch of land that hadn't been claimed by more than one miner. The legal hassle of getting a clear title to build a home was too much for most banks to touch, not to mention the liability of someone getting hurt in one of the abandoned mines.

We had been driving on a washed-out dirt trail of a road for several miles when we spotted Alec's truck. It was parked in the middle of the road with both doors open. Fred couldn't wait to get out of my Jeep and nearly pushed Bonnie out the minute she opened her door. He wasted no time in finding a suitable tree to relieve himself.

"Sorry about that, Bonnie," I said. "I guess the ride was too much on his kidneys."

Bonnie unbuckled her seat belt and turned toward me. The worry lines in her face made her look twenty years older than her sixty-eight years. "Where could he be, Jake?" she asked. Evidently she wasn't the least upset about Fred's hasty exit. "There's nothing here. Why would he come all the way out here?"

"You mean they don't you?" I answered.

She had started to get out of the truck, but stopped to face me again. "They? You think he came with a friend?"

"Not a friend. Both those doors are open. I suppose Alec could have done that, but I don't think so. My guess is Alec left the truck in a big hurry, like he was trying to get away from his passenger."

Bonnie was out her door and headed toward Alec's truck before I finished speaking. Sixty something smokers and drinkers aren't supposed to be so quick, especially at this altitude. My home in Evergreen was close to eight thousand feet and this place had to be a thousand feet higher. She went to the driver's side of the truck and screamed.

Anyone within a mile could have heard her, but I doubt if anyone other than Fred and I did. The place was too remote and inaccessible to get to. "What is it, Bonnie?" I asked when I caught up to her, but before she could answer, Fred came out of nowhere and started barking and growling. I saw a huge raccoon jump out of the truck and run toward an open mine. Fred was right on its tail.

The raccoon knocked Bonnie off her feet in its haste to escape. I yelled out for Fred to come back and went over to Bonnie. "Are you okay?" I asked.

To my relief, she started laughing. "I don't know which is worse. The raccoon or that big ox of yours," she managed between laughs.

It was contagious. I couldn't help it and started laughing too. "My God, Bon, I thought you had found a dead body or something," I said while helping her to her feet.

She brushed off the dirt from her pants. "Damn it," she said, looking at a rip in her pants. "These were my best pair of jeans." The ground was covered in mine tailings that had small, gravel rocks embedded in the dirt.

"Better your jeans than your skin, Bon. Lucky you weren't wearing shorts," I said before calling out for Fred again.

"You're wasting your breath," she said. Then, without skipping a beat, she changed the subject. "I wonder what Alec was doing with a raccoon? Do you think that's why he left the doors open? To get the critter out of his truck?"

"No, I don't think so. I think the raccoon came along later when it smelled those chips," I answered, pointing to a bag of Cheetos scattered across the floor.

The laughter in her voice disappeared, and so did the joyfulness in her face. "I almost forgot about Alec. Do you have a flashlight? I think we should search this mine." she said, pointing toward the hole Fred had gone into.

The mine's entrance had been dug into the side of the hill over a hundred years ago. Alec had parked his truck just below it. Judging by the pile of tailings that had been dug out of the mine and dumped where we were now standing, I estimated that the mine couldn't be more than a few hundred feet deep.

Bonnie didn't wait for me to fetch the flashlight. She was already at the mine's entrance by the time I caught up with her. "What's that terrible smell?" she asked.

I nearly started laughing again. She was holding her nose to illustrate her remark. It was the kind of gesture my daughter made when she had cleaned up after Fred when he was a puppy. It brought back some happy memories.

"Smells like ammonia," I answered. "Or maybe there's a dead animal in there. Better let me go in first, Bon. If it's a dead animal, there could be some scavengers in there who might not like being cornered."

"Oh my God," she said and started yelling while rushing into the mine. "Alec, are you in there, honey?"

It was all I could do to get ahead of her with the flashlight. "Hold up, Bonnie. Please let me go first."

I couldn't see anything that could have caused the smell; no dead animals, no Alec, and even more amazing — no Fred. The mine was much smaller than I had first thought. I didn't even need the flashlight to see. It wasn't more than ten feet deep and the daylight filled every cubic inch of the place. It didn't make sense. There was a small mountain of tailings outside, enough to fill the mine several times over. Then I saw why. The back wall wasn't a wall at all. It was a pile of boulders and dirt blocking access to the rest of the mine behind it.

Bonnie had seen it too, and realized what had happened. "Is that a cave-in, Jake? Oh, God, please don't tell me Alec is behind that."

I didn't answer right away. Something wasn't right. "Fred! Come here boy," I called out. I could see it wasn't a cave-in. The ceiling above the rocks was intact. Those rocks had been placed there by someone who was hiding something.

Within seconds, Fred poked his head through a small space at the top of the rock pile. "Get your butt down here, Mister," I said then turned to Bonnie. "Please stay put this time, Bon. I'll crawl up there and see what's behind that pile."

"Alec!" she called out as loud as she could. "Are you back there, Alec?"

Alec didn't answer, but Fred did. Instead of obeying my order to come down from his perch, he barked at me then went back behind the pile of rubble. It was obvious he wanted me to follow.

This time I didn't give Bonnie a chance to get ahead of me. I was up and over the boulders before she could respond. Fred was waiting for me on the other side. Once he saw me hit the ground, he ran off into the mine. Maybe he could see, but now that the sun was all but blocked out, I paused to turn on my flashlight. The mine did continue on for another hundred feet or so, just as I had originally thought. I swept my light in a slow semi-circle. There weren't any dead animals or scavengers, and to my relief, no sign of Alec either.

"It's okay, Bon," I yelled back to her. "He's not here." Then I saw what Fred was so excited about. "Oh, shit," I said in a much lower tone. Hopefully low enough that Bonnie couldn't hear.

There were propane bottles, burners, cans of acetone and white-gas everywhere. One of the propane bottles must have been leaking and I could tell it wasn't propane.

It was the stench of ammonia. Fred had discovered a meth lab.

"What is it, Jake?" Bonnie asked. She was at the top of the rock pile.

"Don't come down, Bonnie. You might not make it back up. The rocks on this side are treacherous."

"Then tell me what all that stuff is before I come down to see for myself."

"It looks like Alec's meth lab," I answered. I reached out and touched a big pan on top of a camp stove. "And by the feel of this, he hasn't been here in a while." Then I saw Bonnie starting down the pile of rocks.

"Wait there, Bonnie. I'm coming up before I pass out from these fumes."

She surprised me this time and did as I asked and went back outside to wait for me. She was sitting in Alec's truck, smoking a cigarette when I joined her.

"Where could he have gone, Jake?"

"I wish I knew. Maybe Fred can tell us," I answered while watching Fred sniffing the ground in front of Alec's truck.

She flicked her cigarette to the ground and bent down to Fred's level, "Can you do that for your Aunt Bonnie, Freddie?" Her voice was breaking up. Tears were not far behind.

Fred seemed to understand. He turned and went back to sniffing the ground.

"I think he's found something," I said, pointing to the tracks Fred was checking out. The ground was still barren and easily disturbed wherever there were tailings. Nothing could grow in the fine gravel and decomposed granite.

Bonnie looked up at me and wiped her face. "Why do they go away from the mine, Jake?"

Fred looked back at us and smiled, then put his nose to the ground to follow the tracks. Well, it looked like he was smiling. It's hard to tell with Goldens. They're always happy.

"You're right, Bon. They don't go into the mine. Looks like Fred smells something going off toward those trees over there." I pointed in the direction Fred was heading. The tracks disappeared in the thin grass once they left the area around the mine.

Fred stopped acting like a bloodhound and picked up a small stick from a clump of weeds.

"Once a retriever always a retriever," I said to Bonnie.

"That's not a stick, Jake," she said, going out to see what he had. "Its Alec's knife!"

The fear and tone of her voice made Fred's tail disappear between his legs. He dropped his prize at her feet. The big sissy thought he was in trouble. I hurried over to them and picked up the knife.

"It's okay, Freddie," I said, petting him on the head. "Aunt Bonnie's not mad at you. You did good. Real good."

The knife wasn't anything you could buy at your local Walmart. I had seen my father use a knife just like it years ago to skin a deer, and by the looks of it, this knife had been used to skin something. It was covered in dried-out blood.

"I bought it for his birthday at Cabela's. I had to drive all the way up to Thornton to get it for him," she said then screamed when she saw the blood.

"He's dead, isn't he, Jake?" she asked, grabbing me around the waist.

"We don't know that, Bon," I said while rubbing her shoulders in a feeble attempt to comfort her. Then I held her by both shoulders and forced her to look me in the eyes. "It's probably from some animal. Meth isn't the only thing Alec's been up to. I'll bet my next paycheck, there's a bear or elk around here missing some vital organs."

"You think he's the poacher?" she asked, breaking away from my grasp and walking toward Alec's truck.

She acted confused or angry. I couldn't tell which. Maybe it was both. Fred must have felt it too. He followed her to the truck and tried to get her attention by rubbing up against her legs. When she bent down to pet him, I could see she was crying.

"I'm sorry, Bon. I never seem to know when to keep my big mouth shut," I said while walking over to her and Fred. I felt like a little kid again when I told my mother the truth after she had asked me if her new dress made her look fat.

"I know, Jake," she answered without taking her eyes off Fred. He was really playing it up by moving his head so she would rub his ears now that he had her attention. "But what if it is his blood? What if he's laying dead in that mine. Where is he?"

"He's not in the mine. I swept my light over every square inch of that place. I also didn't see any fresh tracks in the tailings outside the mine," I answered, bending down on one knee to pet Fred while looking Bonnie in the face.

"How can you be so sure?"

"Our footprints are sharp and crisp. All the others are barely noticeable."

She was really upset now. She was actually shaking. "Not the tracks. How can you be so sure he's not in there?"

I stood up and reached out for her hand, pretending to steady myself, but really in an attempt to comfort her. "Alec didn't go into that mine, at least not recently. Think about it, Bon. Both the truck doors left open and his phone on the floor. It looks like he was trying to get away from whoever was in the passenger seat. Kids now days wouldn't leave their smart phones behind unless they were running for their lives. Why don't you go back to my Jeep while me and Fred search the area on the other side of those weeds where he found the knife?"

The way she squeezed my hand told me her answer before she said it. "No way, Jake. I'm going with you boys and that's that."

It didn't take long to pick up the trail again once we came on another mine. This one was only an exploratory hole, not a real mine, but the tailings around it had fresh footprints. Alec and someone else had been running. The distance between the prints was too great for walking. It looked like Alec ran for thirty feet or so past the tailings and headed toward a gulley another fifty yards away. We found the prints again in some grass just before the gulley. They had to be recent, for the grass, or what passed as grass at this elevation, was still laying flat. I couldn't actually see footprints, but the bent grass was all I needed. Fred saw, or smelled them, too. He took off toward the gulley like a fox on the scent of a rabbit, which is how Fred found Alec.

Chapter 13

It was totally dark by the time the mountain rescue team lifted Alec from the pit and secured him in the helicopter. Bonnie and I would have been two more victims of the open mine shaft if Fred hadn't found it first. His sixth sense, or maybe his close proximity to the ground, had seen the nearly invisible hole before we could fall into it like Alec had. It was another exploratory hole dug by a miner over a hundred years ago. Those holes were required back then in order to stake a claim. Brush had grown up around the hole in those hundred years or so making the mine a death trap to the careless. Alec had fallen twenty feet straight down. The only thing that saved him was a pile of old tires someone had dumped in the hole. There was no one else. Whoever had been chasing Alec must have seen him fall and ran away long before we arrived.

I didn't get a helicopter ride to the hospital with Alec and Bonnie. I had the privilege of being interrogated by Clear Creek's finest on what we were doing there. The search team had found the meth lab and the sheriff's deputy in charge was sure I had something to do with it. I would be sitting in a cell in Idaho Springs right now if not for Fred. The deputy felt sorry for Fred, or so he said, knowing he would be taken to an animal shelter if they locked me up. Once the deputy confirmed we had no prior drug convictions, or any wants or warrants against us, we were allowed to go our own way with the cliché of being told not to leave town.

Without a television to watch or light to read a book by, I decided to do a little research on the knife later that night. While browsing a web page on hunting knives, I ran across an interesting article on hunting bows. Like most web searches, I was led down a path that had nothing to do with knives, but it did confirm what I already suspected. Jonathan and Alec were the prime suspects for poaching.

I had been diverted to a page on bows and archery. Unlike guns, it's pretty hard to trace bows and there are few restrictions on who can own one, but I remembered Julie said it was an expensive custom bow. It didn't take long to find that the better compound bow manufacturers' number each one that they made. That was no earthshaking revelation. I'd look pretty foolish pointing a finger at the father and son team based on that. Then I searched for Jonathan plus archery and found a news clipping on Jonathan placing in a local archery competition. I was pretty sure Julie could do a DNA match on the bear remains, and the blood on Alec's knife. It was also a good bet she could trace the bow they found in my motor home to Jonathan as well. I'd not only get Chuck off my back, but I'd collect that thousand dollar reward too.

Fred and I returned to the crime scene later the next day after visiting Alec at the hospital. Bonnie, Margot and Jonathan had spent the night, keeping a vigil over Alec. The poor kid was in a coma. It was the first time I'd seen him without his nose and lip rings. The nurses had removed those to put tubes down his throat. It wasn't the time to ask Margot to get Chuck to drop his lawsuit. That would require me to explain why I thought Alec was an accomplice to the poaching. I wasn't quite ready to point out the poaching mastermind, not with him in the room.

Returning to the mine had seemed like a good idea at the time. Now I wasn't so sure. The ride up the mountain was too much for my old Jeep. Water was gushing out from under the hood and the engine kept trying to go on its own long after I had shut it off.

I was cussing at my Wagoneer when Fred went into his attack mode with his ears back and the hair along his spine standing straight up. Something, or someone, had spooked him. He was walking in a crouching position toward the mine when all of a sudden his ears went up and his hair down and he began wagging his tail. He was off into the mine like a cat after a mouse. "Get back here, Fred," I yelled too late. "There could be a bear in there." Then I saw why he was so happy.

Julie was coming out of the mine and bent down to rub Fred's head. "I know I can be grumpy at times, Jake, but I've never been accused of being a bear."

The afternoon light made her hair seem redder than I remembered. She had just taken off her warden's cap to shake her hair loose. I suppose it was to rid herself of imaginary bats or bugs. The supermodels on the cover of Vogue would kill to look the way she did just now.

"More like Goldilocks, if you ask me," I answered. "What are you doing up here all by yourself? Aren't you afraid the big bad wolf might get you?"

She stood up from petting Fred and smiled. "Got your fairy tales a little mixed up, don't you? That was Little Red Riding Hood the wolf was after, but I should be safe now that the fearless woodsman has arrived."

Her smile was infectious. My mood changed instantly and I completely forgot about my own problems. All I could think of was what a fool I had been to let her get away.

"How have you been, Julie?" I asked after I made my way over to her and my dog.

"It's only been a couple days," she answered. The smile had faded. "How have you guys been?"

"Sad," I answered. "And foolish, you're the best thing that's happened to me in years. I really miss you."

"Then shut up and kiss me, Jake. I missed you too."

We left my ailing Wagoneer behind and rode into town in the state issued SUV she had parked out of sight behind a pile of mine tailings. I assumed it was a habit wildlife agents developed to hide from their prey. It explained why she had surprised me coming out of the mine. I never once gave a thought to Bonnie or Alec after the first kiss. Julie had me in her spell and I was enjoying every moment with her.

We found an old, pet-friendly, motel along the river in Idaho Springs and now we were famished. It must have been all the energy spent from making love in the middle of the afternoon. I waited outside by the river with Fred while Julie got ready to go into town.

It always amazed me how most women wouldn't think of leaving the house without their makeup. Julie not only carried her makeup with her, she also kept a change of clothes in her SUV for emergencies like this. At least that's what she said. Being of a completely different gender, Fred and I didn't even bother to bring a razor when we left the house. Not that he would know how to use one anyway.

Fred was lucky enough to clean up in the river; whereas, I would have to hope I didn't offend Julie with my now sweaty and dusty clothes. Watching him weave his way across the shallow water by choosing just the right rocks to step on, gave me the time I needed to collect my thoughts. I wanted to tell her how much I loved her no matter how bad the cancer got. Neither one of us had broached that subject yet. I decided she would tell me when she was ready.

I also had to find a way to ask Julie to run a check on the bow she had found in my motor home. Asking for a

DNA test on the knife would have to wait. If the bow did indeed belong to Jonathan, she would have a good reason to run the expensive DNA test.

I was coming up with more questions than a game show host when she emerged from the room wearing shorts and a Colorado Rockies tee shirt. Her attire was topped off with a matching cap. How she got all that stuff in one little overnight bag would puzzle Houdini.

We couldn't put Fred back into the room until he dried off or Julie would have to smell wet dog-hair along with my clothes all night. So I made a makeshift leash out of some rope Julie had in her SUV and we took him with us while we strolled along Miner Street looking into all the antique stores and checking out the menus posted outside several restaurants. I think Fred was becoming jealous. Every time I would take Julie's hand in mine, he would butt his big head between us, wrapping the rope around my legs. I finally got tired of being tripped by the big ox and wound the rope into a small loop and gave it to him so he could walk himself. It didn't take long before we had a small crowd watching us.

Julie thought it was cute that Fred could walk himself. He strutted behind us like the leash was attached to my hand, but of course it wasn't. We would stop to look into a store window, and Fred would sit by my feet with the rope-leash in his mouth. When we went to look into another window, he wasn't more than the distance of the rope behind even though he was free to take off chasing cars or cats whenever he wanted.

"This looks good," Julie said, pointing to a menu posted outside Beau Jo's. "Have you ever had one of their mountain pies?"

"No, but it sounds great," I lied. It had been one of my ex-wife's favorites.

Julie knelt down and patted Fred's head. "Somehow I don't think he'll be welcome at our table," she said, looking up at me while rubbing Fred behind his ears with both her hands.

"Well, technically, he is on a leash so I wouldn't be breaking any laws by leaving him here," I answered.

Julie looked up just in time to catch the flash of someone's camera. People were now taking pictures of the cute dog carrying his own leash.

"Something tells me there's going to be a regular circus crowd if you leave him out here. Why don't you take him back to the room and I'll go in and order?" Then she kissed me on the cheek and disappeared into the restaurant.

"I guess we got our orders, Freddie," I said, turning to face him. He didn't look up. He just kept posing for the crowd. I swear he was smiling.

"Come on you mangy mutt. Let's get you back to the room and if you behave yourself, I'll bring you back some dinner."

Going back to the room alone with Fred turned out to be an eye opener. Julie had left her overnight bag open on the bed. I don't like to consider myself a snoop, but it was like she had left it there for me, or should I say, Fred? He went straight for the case. There was a half-eaten bag of corn chips on top of some papers. Fred pushed the papers aside and helped himself to the chips.

"Fred!" I yelled. "That's not ours. Give it to me."

Fred must have known he was in trouble. He immediately dropped the bag of chips and lowered his head to avoid looking at me. I quickly picked up the package and examined it for dog spittle. The outside was a little wet, but the chips inside were untouched. I took out a couple pieces and threw it to him.

"Guess she won't miss those," I said, patting him on the head.

The chips disappeared in a millisecond. Fred looked up at me expecting more now that he could see I wasn't really mad.

"No way, Jose." I turned my back to him and began picking up the papers he had scattered in his haste to get at the chips. "What the hell?" I couldn't believe my eyes. The papers were from Ray's manuscript.

What was Julie doing with the manuscript? Did Margot give it to her, and if so, why? My mind was racing, trying to work out how and why Julie had Ray's book. I quickly checked the page numbers; they started at page two, twenty-three and ended ten pages later. My scanner had jammed on page two twenty-two. With the exception of that one page, I now had the entire manuscript.

My first impulse was to sit down and read where I had left off. Then I had an epiphany. I took my cell phone from my pocket and started to take pictures of the pages. It didn't take long. I took snapshots of two at a time. Maybe I would discover why Julie had the manuscript when I had the chance to read them later.

I put everything back the best I could and left for the restaurant after telling Fred to guard the fort.

"Looks like Fred's going to have a treat," Julie said, nodding toward the leftovers. She had ordered us a pitcher of gluten-free beer and a mountain pie with pepperoni, sausage, and artichoke hearts. The artichokes were okay; however, most of the beer went untouched. The mountain pie on the other hand was fantastic. It was huge. The crust was so thick that we ate it for desert by squirting honey on it. It was a meal in itself.

"If Fred drinks all that beer he's going to have to join alcohol anonymous," I said. "Besides, I don't think they'll let us take it back to the room."

"The pizza, Goofy," she answered with a huge grin. "But he's going to have to fight me for the crust. I'd forgotten how good it is."

For some stupid reason, I couldn't take my eyes off her smile. I should have been thinking how beautiful it made her look, but all I could think of was how much someone must have paid for such beautiful teeth. They were perfect and must have cost a fortune. This I knew from the dentist bill I was still paying for my daughter.

"Earth to Jake. Are you still with me?"

I quickly glanced down at the pizza; embarrassed for staring at her. "Speaking of Fred, he sort of made a mess of your suitcase."

She didn't even blink. "He found the corn chips, I take it."

"And the manuscript," I answered, looking into her eyes again.

She looked at me like I had dementia or something. "You missed the camera?" she asked.

Now I was the one who was confused. "The camera? What camera?"

"Guess I left it in the car. I must be getting senile in my old age."

"I can think of plenty of things you haven't forgotten," I said, reaching out to take her free hand in mine. "You still know how to turn a guy into putty."

"If that was putty you had an hour ago, I'd hate to see the real thing," she answered, squeezing my hands. "But seriously, Jake, you can't tell anyone about the camera or the manuscript. They're both part of the investigation and I'd get in a lot of trouble if anyone finds out I let you see them."

Then it dawned on me. "So that's why you were in that mine. Why on earth did you have one of your cameras in there?" I asked, freeing her hand from my grasp.

"I have no idea what you're talking about, Jake," she answered, smiling again. "Now suppose I had placed a camera up there and suppose that instead of discovering a poacher, I saw someone making meth. You don't think I would be able to share that information with you, do you? I could compromise a major investigation if I ever told you we had known about Alec's operation for some time and that we were waiting to see who else was involved."

"Then you know who chased Alec into the other mine shaft?" I asked.

She looked around the restaurant before answering. A Hispanic guy at the bar turned away almost on cue. "Maybe once I download the SIM card. The camera couldn't talk to our server from inside the mine." Her voice was barely audible.

She checked on our friend at the bar before continuing. "But I can't tell you that, Jake, anymore than I can tell you the DA is thinking about charging you for negligent homicide."

"Negligent homicide? For what?" Her statement made me forget all about asking how she came by the manuscript.

"Causing Lonnie's death; that's a class 5 felony in Colorado, punishable with one to four years in prison."

"That's bullshit! Everyone knows it was an accident."

"Chuck has friends in high places, Jake. Whatever did you do to piss him off? On second thought, I don't want to know. I never told you about the DA. Remember? But if you were to do a little reading tonight after we fall asleep, assuming we sleep, you might find more than you bargained for." She reached out to take my hand in hers. "It's been a long day. What say we take Fred his dinner?"

I didn't tell Julie about the deal Chuck tried to make at the Little Bear. At the time I thought he was just trying to get me to sign his stupid affidavit. It was time to play my trump card and call Margot in the morning. In the meantime, I had to think of a tactful way to remind her Alec owed me his life.

It was well past two in the morning by the time I got around to do the "little reading" Julie had suggested. I read with disbelief while sitting in a corner chair with Fred at my feet. The dim light from a table lamp didn't seem to stop Julie or Fred from their dreams. Julie had fallen asleep in my arms and I had slowly extricated myself from her grasp so as not to wake her. Now I sat quietly, trying to make sense of what I had just read while watching her sleep.

Ray had known about the mine for years. He had bought the claim back in the sixties for only five hundred dollars. Either Jonathan or Alec had read Ray's manuscript. Either that, or maybe the old man simply told them about his claim. In any case, at least now I knew why Alec had chosen that particular spot to set up a meth lab. He didn't have to worry about the owner making a surprise visit; Ray couldn't object and neither Bonnie nor Margot had reason to visit the site.

I finally understood why Margot wanted her father's manuscript back. Ray had switched from trying to tell a story to an autobiography. At the end he no longer tried to hide his guilt in fictional characters. He claimed Chuck had an affair with Margot when they were much younger. Margot and Chuck were both married at the time, just not to each other. Ray suspected Jonathan was really Chuck's son, which made Alec his grandson. Ray's brilliant deduction had been based on the knowledge that Margot's husband had a vasectomy during his first marriage.

It was no wonder Margot and Chuck were so upset with Alec and Marissa making out, and why she wanted the manuscript back. I couldn't help but wonder if Bonnie knew the two kids were cousins. Their kissing didn't seem to bother her in the least.

Poor Margot must have popped a hemorrhoid when she realized she gave me the original. I wish I could have seen her face when she did. At least now I knew why Chuck wanted my copy so badly, but it didn't explain why he wanted to nail me to the cross. You would think he'd be kissing my butt hoping I would keep my mouth shut. It's not smart to harass someone who knows your dirty family secrets.

Ray's book was great gossip, but nothing to kill over. Lonnie wasn't even mentioned in it. It also wasn't going to help me with my Chuck problem.

I was sure of one thing. Lonnie's death was no accident. The hose to the propane tank had been tampered with. Someone had rigged the hose to leak either before or during the barbeque. Unfortunately, I was the only one who believed Lonnie had been murdered. His demise was officially listed as an accident, and if Chuck got his way it would become a negligent homicide with me as the drunk who caused the accident.

So there I was, sitting in a worn-out, overstuffed armchair, watching a beautiful game-warden sleep and trying to make sense of her involvement in a case that had nothing to do with wild animals. What was her connection to all this? I could have sat there until the sun came up, but Fred suddenly woke up and started to growl.

"What's the matter, Boy?" I whispered. "Dreaming about cats again?"

He answered with a loud bark and ran to the door.

"Jake?" Julie was wide awake now. Instinctively, she pulled the blankets over her naked breasts.

"Shh," I answered while quickly grabbing my jeans and shirt. "I think someone is out there by your car. Hold Fred and I'll go check."

Julie scrambled for her clothes with one hand and took Fred's collar with the other.

"On second thought, let him come with me," I said, opening the door a crack.

Fred wasted no time pushing me out of the way and running out the door toward Julie's car. She had parked it some fifty or sixty yards from the room. All the close-in spots were taken at the time, but it was still within eyesight of our room. I could see the interior light on and then heard a door slam and the light go off. Fred covered the fifty yards in greyhound time. He was on the intruder before the guy could get away. I was closing the gap when I saw the jerk give Fred a sharp kick in the side. Fred had been trying to bite the guy's leg, but let out a yelp and let the guy go after the kick. I was too late. By the time I reached Fred, his assailant was already in his car and speeding out of the parking lot. Fred wasn't moving.

"Is he okay?" It was Julie. She had managed to throw on some clothes and come running out behind me.

I reached for the spot where Fred had been kicked and he instantly yelped. "No," I answered, "it looks like he may have some internal injury." Then, as an afterthought, I added, "Watch where you walk. There's glass everywhere."

Julie pushed me aside and bent down to pet Fred on the head. "It's okay, Freddie," she said. "Aunt Julie is just going to take a look. I promise I won't hurt you."

Fred looked into her eyes as though he understood every word. He watched while she slowly moved her hand from his head, down his back and to his side. This time he only flinched a little and didn't yelp.

"Looks like a bruised rib," she said. "It will probably be okay, but we should get him to the vet and have it x-rayed just the same."

Several of the other guests had come to their doors by now and were watching us. None of them wanted to leave the safety of their rooms and didn't venture past the threshold. I knew it wouldn't be long before the police showed up.

"Good idea," I answered. "Do you mind getting our bags while I carry Fred into the back seat? I know an emergency animal clinic in town that should be open by the time we get there, but we've got to go now." I didn't want to be detained by the men in blue when my dog could be bleeding internally.

She ignored me and opened the door of her SUV. "Damn it!" she yelled. "He got the camera."

Chapter 14

"You're going to be okay, Freddie" Julie said from the back seat while I drove her SUV down Interstate Seventy. I was tempted to see how fast the big car would go, but stayed within the speed limit. Being stopped by the Colorado State Patrol was the last thing we needed. They might ask too many questions, like why the car's window is broken.

The rear-view mirror was set for Julie's shorter frame and gave me a view of the rear seat instead of the road. She was holding Fred like a mother would hold a sick child. His head was resting on her lap and she patted it softly.

"I think I know who did it, if that helps," I said to the mirror.

"Oh?"

"Remember that guy trying to listen in our conversation?"

"At Beau Jo's?"

"I think he works for Jonathan."

She stopped petting Fred long enough to look me in the eyes via the mirror. Her face was a combination of surprise and fear. "He must have followed us from the mine," she said.

"And I'll bet your camera has his picture inside the mine, probably making meth. Too bad you didn't have one outside as well."

"Maybe he thinks I did. Do you think he could be the one who chased Alec into the open pit?"

"I don't know," I answered. "You're a cop. Can't you have him brought in and pistol whipped until he confesses?"

"Funny, Jake. You should go on the Tonight show." She had gone back to petting Fred and answered me in between talking baby-talk to him. "I think I told you it was out of my hands, didn't I? The joint task force took over after I reported the lab."

"No, nor did you say why you were up there in the first place. Not that it's any of my business, but I'm dying to know."

"You're right. It's none of your business, but I've always had a soft spot for cute dogs, so I'll tell Fred."

The big ham looked up at her at the mention of his name.

"I hid the camera there after receiving an anonymous tip, Freddie."

"Lonnie called the hot line?" I asked.

"Wow, Fred, what a deep voice you have."

"All the better to eat you with, my Dear," I answered.

"You really need to get a handle on your fairy tales, Jake. Now where we, Freddie, before we were interrupted? No. it wasn't Lonnie. Someone left a note on my windshield, but that's between us, okay? She told us where to look. We couldn't really stake the place out without being seen. It was too remote, so I went there to place a game camera in the mine, hoping to catch Jonathan with his pants down."

"You caught Jonathan taking off his clothes?" I joked, trying to get her to smile again.

I could see her reflection in the mirror. She tried not to smile, but failed miserably. "You know what I mean, Goofy."

"Then the meth lab is something fairly recent? And how do you know the concerned citizen was female?" I asked the mirror.

She was still petting Fred and talking to him, but stopped long enough to answer me. "Pink sticky notes with perfect handwriting had to be a woman; and no, the lab was set up before I placed the camera. Anyway, that's when I called the sheriff, who brought in the task force." Evidently the charade of telling Fred was over. She was looking at me in the mirror. Fred didn't care. I could tell the big mutt was eating up all the attention she was giving him. His tail was starting to thump; it was a good sign that the kick hadn't done any real damage.

Before I could ask what they had seen on the game camera, I saw flashing red lights in the distance from the side mirror. We were coming up on the Genesee exit so I made a split-second decision to get off the freeway. I knew old highway forty paralleled the interstate and would take me all the way to ninety-three where I could get back on the freeway, then on to Ward Road where the vet was located. I adjusted the rear-view mirror to get a better look behind me just in time to see the red lights disappear in a dip in the road. Hopefully, the cop, if that's what it was, wouldn't see me exit.

"Why are you getting off here, Jake?" Julie asked.

"I thought I'd drive past the Mother Cabrini shrine. No time to go up there, but we can always say a prayer for Fred as we drive by."

"I doubt if it's a cop, Jake, but turn on the radio. The last button is the State Patrol frequency." She had seen through my paranoia.

I reached over to turn on the radio. It didn't work. Then I noticed wires dangling under the dash. "Looks like he did more than steal your camera, Julie. This guy is smart. He made sure you couldn't call it in as well."

She took her eyes off Fred long enough to stick her head between the two front seats. Fred was having none of it and tried to slip in between. "Damn. I've got some explaining to do on what I was doing in Idaho Springs."

By now we were on the overpass. Julie was right. The red lights belonged to an ambulance. I pulled over and watched it go down Interstate Seventy. When I turned back from watching the ambulance, I saw Julie watching me with her beautiful green eyes.

"You could tell them you were celebrating your engagement." I said with a grin.

Her eyes swelled and I could tell she was holding back tears. "Please, Jake. Don't ruin this for us. You know I can't marry you."

"You're not going to die, Julie. You can beat this. You did it once before and you can do it again," I said while trying to reach between the seats to take her hand. "I love you and I'm going to make sure you get through it no matter what."

She couldn't hold back the tears any longer. "Will you still love me when I'm bald or when I can't get out of bed because all I'll want to do is sleep?" she asked, rummaging through her purse for a tissue.

I noticed she kept a small pack of them in a compartment next to the radio and handed her the pack. "You won't be alone. If the chemo makes your hair fall out, Fred and I will cut ours too. If you want to sleep all day, we'll be there the minute you wake up. Please, Julie, please say you'll marry me." I should have kept some of the tissues for now I could feel tears in my eyes.

"You would do that for me?"

"If you will have us," I answered, nodding toward Fred, who seemed to have made a full recovery. He must have understood as well. His tail was wagging faster than a nervous rattlesnake. "I know we don't have much to offer, but I promise with him around, you'll never get bored."

Julie grabbed the back of my head and pulled me toward her to kiss me. I could taste her salty tears. I tried to kiss her back but a huge furry lump between us would have no part of it and started to bark.

We celebrated our engagement at my little cabin. The x-rays confirmed what I already knew. Fred had no broken bones or internal injuries. He made a miraculous recovery after I had proposed to Julie. Whoever said dogs were dumb animals didn't know my Freddie. He understood better than most children that Julie was going to be his new mom.

Except to let Fred out when he got bored with us, we didn't leave the cabin for two days. I was beginning to think she was some kind of international spy because of the way she got me to open up and tell her all my secrets. Just like the beautiful women in the movies, she knew exactly when to pump me for more information. By Monday, she knew the story of my life, including all the juicy details of my nasty divorce. All I got from her was how she came upon the manuscript. It was in the dumpster along with her broken camera at Randolph Motors.

Julie called in sick on Monday. It wasn't because of fatigue or fever, even though that's what she told someone at the office. By Tuesday she felt bad for lying and had to go to work. She gave me a ride back to my Jeep, then followed me to Evergreen Parkway in case it broke down again. I honked and blew her a kiss, then turned south toward home. Fred probably would have done the same if he could. Instead, he jumped in the back and watched Julie turn onto the freeway.

"Well, Freddie, how about I buy you a McDouble? Will that cheer you up?" I asked while switching to the left lane to make my turn into McDonald's. "But you've got to promise not to tell your new mother. She doesn't think you should be eating them."

I pulled into the drive-up lane, then quickly pulled out and found a parking spot next to a red Bronco. I couldn't imagine what Bonnie was doing at McDonald's, but it seemed like a good time to tell her about my engagement and ask about Alec. "Wait here, Freddie. I'll only be a moment," I said while cranking his window down halfway.

Once inside, I searched for Bonnie. When I didn't see her at any of the tables, I guessed she was in the ladies' room so I placed an order for two burgers and a coffee. She still hadn't come out by the time my order was ready, so I took a seat by the restrooms and sipped on my coffee while looking at the silent television on the wall. A Fox reporter was trying to make a case against the lack of security in Benghazi by showing footage from a surveillance camera. It might as well have been a movie about aliens for all I could see were dark-green figures with bright eyes reflecting the light of the infrared security camera. I soon tired of the scene and began to ponder my future with Julie.

Would she want a full-blown wedding or settle for a quickie civil ceremony? She had told me she had been married before in a big church ceremony. That marriage broke up less than six months later when she caught her husband in bed with his best friend. She said it was a shock and forgave him, but he decided he liked his friend better than her and that was the end of their short marriage. The marriage was annulled, so it was conceivable she might want to try another church wedding. I was about to give up on Bonnie, realizing that there could be more than one beat-up Bronco in these parts, when a pretty teenage girl came out of the ladies' room. The thing that caught my attention, other than her good looks, was that she was a dead ringer for Molly Ringwald in the movie Pretty in Pink. Then it hit me. In an instant, I knew who tipped off Julie about the poaching. The image of Shelia at the hospital dressed in pink was too vivid to ignore.

I was about ready to take Fred his burgers when Bonnie appeared from nowhere. To be honest, she had probably followed Molly from the restroom, but I was too engrossed in Ms. Ringwald to notice.

"Jake, did you hear!" She was beaming from ear to ear. "Alec came out of his coma. I'm on my way down there now."

"That's great Bon," I answered and got up to hug her. "Is there anything I can do to help?"

"Keep praying for him. He's going to need all the prayers he can get," she answered after hugging me back. "I know he wouldn't be here otherwise."

"You got it, Bon." I really wanted to ask if Alec had told anyone what he was doing at the mine, but decided that would have to wait.

"I've gotta go, Jake. I'll call you later," she said and hurried out the door.

Bonnie wasn't out of the parking lot before I was on the phone to Julie.

Chapter 15

"How did you know, Jake?" Julie asked after she told me about Alec's confession. She was sitting in my ex-wife's Queen Anne chair with nothing on but my bathrobe after taking a long shower. I really needed to get rid of that chair.

"Elementary, my dear Watson. When I realized it was Shelia who tipped you off about the mine, I thought to myself, 'Why did she do it anonymously?' The only reason I could think of is that she had to be afraid of the repercussions and she didn't want the poacher to know it was her. At first I thought it was Jonathan and she was afraid he would turn her in for driving the Corvette the night Diane was killed, but he's had over twenty years to do that so it had to be someone else. Then out of nowhere I made a connection with Benghazi and your security camera."

"Benghazi? I'm afraid you lost me, Jake," she said, looking at me like I'd lost my marbles.

"Yeah. Me too. I mean it always amazes me the way the mind works, or the way my mind works. The point is that every time a gun would go off I could see the flash from the infrared light reflection and I knew in an instant what caused those spots in your game camera picture. It wasn't a dirty lens. It was puffs of smoke coming from the getaway vehicle."

Julie continued to stare, looking more bewildered than before, so I went on before she had a chance to ask if I'd been smoking Bonnie's homemade cigarettes.

"Jonathan's crew drove a truck that belched white smoke whenever it shifted gears. It confirmed my suspicion that Jonathan and Alec were doing the poaching. I mean, think about it. Jonathan is an excellent archer and he had his roofing crew to do all his dirty work."

I had to pause to pinch myself. Julie was so cute the way she sat there asking questions. I found it very hard to concentrate, but went on anyway. "All you needed to wrap up the case was some proof. That's when I suggested you try to make a deal with Alec."

Julie picked up a brush she had brought from the bathroom and ran it through her hair several times before speaking. "Well, Sherlock, you just about nailed it. Except for Jonathan being involved, your guess was pretty good. Alec claims his father had no knowledge of the poaching or the meth lab. He's trying to put all the blame on Mario and his crew, claiming it was Mario who chased him into the open pit when he tried to run away because he was afraid Mario was going to kill him."

I watched while she brushed her hair and caught myself wondering what she'd look like bald. "So what happens to Alec now?" I asked.

"I'm sure the DA will either drop the making and distributing charge or at least reduce it to possession if he continues to help us."

"And Mario and his crew? I can't wait until you interrogate them. I'm sure it was one of them who followed us from the mine when we went into Idaho Springs."

"Me too. My boss is still pissed about the broken radio and window, but Alec did tell us why Mario didn't take his truck after chasing him into the hole. Alec had the keys in his pocket."

"Will you follow up on why he was working at Randolph Motors? I'm sure Chuck is involved too."

"That's all out of my hands."

"But you're still in charge of the poaching prosecution, aren't you?"

She stopped brushing her hair and looked up at me. Her eyes were wet. "No. I put in for a medical leave today. I called my doctor and told him to go ahead and set up the chemotherapy."

Without any hesitation, she dropped her robe on the floor, hitting Fred, who was sleeping at her side. "Come over here and carry me into bed. I need someone to give me a back-rub and tell me how much they love me."

The falling robe woke Fred. He looked up at the naked lady and went right back to sleep. Maybe he wasn't human after all. Without another word, I did as I was told and carried Julie to bed.

"Over to the left a little, Jake. Yeah, right there. God that feels so good," she said in response to my attempt at a massage. "Something tells me you've had practice at this."

I let my hand slide down to the base of her spine. "Are you sure you don't work for the CIA?"

She turned over on her side and slapped my hand. "There'll be plenty of time for that later," she said and turned back on her stomach. "Now get back to work and what ever made you think I could work for the CIA?"

"Well, you surely missed your calling. It seems I'm the one answering all the questions," I said while going back to rubbing her shoulder muscles.

"Keep that up and I'll tell you everything. Now over to the right," she said, twisting her shoulder so I could rub it too.

"I keep coming back to Shelia's motive. If it was the reward she was after, wouldn't she have to tell you her name?"

"Not if she called our hotline. We give a code that can be used to collect the reward once we get a conviction."

"But she didn't call the hotline, so I assume she wasn't after a reward," I said while trying not to let my hands wander. "Shelia's words at the hospital keep coming back to me. She said she would make me pay for Lonnie's death, so maybe she thought I was the one doing the poaching and she wanted you to catch me. When you think about it, she never said it was Jonathan."

"I did catch you, didn't I?" Julie said, rolling to her side to face me.

Nothing can get a man's testosterone level up faster than a naked woman in his bed. My ability to solve any mental puzzle vanished. So I did the next best thing and kissed her. "I think I'm the one who made the catch. By the way, have I told you lately that I love you?"

Once again, it was Fred who woke me from my bliss. I put on the robe Julie had abandoned earlier and let him out. Glancing at the old windup clock on the wall I saw it had stopped at two-twenty. I couldn't remember the last time I wound it so I checked the clock on the DVD player, forgetting my electricity was off. I had jury-rigged my generator to heat and pump water for Julie's shower, but now it was off again.

My cell phone finally confirmed what my four-legged clock had already told me. It was close to sunrise. Julie would be getting up soon to get ready for work and I couldn't decide if I should wake her so we could continue where we left off the night before or let her sleep. I decided on the latter and took my place in the Queen Anne chair.

Fred's scratching at the door woke my sleeping beauty. She looked up at the wall clock with drooping eyes and reached for a pillow. "Wake me up at five,

Mister Hunk, and I'll have time to make us some breakfast before I get ready for work," she said before covering her face with the pillow.

I went over and kissed her on the neck, ignoring Fred's scratching plea to come in. "Don't worry about breakfast. It's after five already. Get some more sleep and I'll have breakfast ready when you get up."

The pillow went flying when Julie bolted upright. "After Five? Christ, I'm going to be late."

Fred had waited for me to make breakfast, but I wasn't in the mood and filled his bowl with dry dog-food before pouring myself the coffee I had tried to share with Julie. She didn't have time to chat and took a cup with her, so now it was just me and Fred; and he had gone back to sleep without taking a single bite of his food. He must have been dining on squirrel in his dreams, for his feet were going while he slept through several phone calls I made.

The first call was to my sister back in Missouri to let her know about my engagement, and to ask for a loan. I had to get the lights turned back on if Julie was going to move in with me. Then I made a couple calls to some old friends to let them know I was ready to go back to work. My writing and handyman jobs would never be enough to pay for her insurance once hers ran out. I needed a job with benefits.

The last call was to Bonnie, but not before placing an ad on Craigslist to sell my motor home. Bonnie claimed she was okay with me calling Julie after I learned Alec had come out of his coma. She told me I had done everyone a big favor because the other cops would have crucified him if not for Julie being there. She went so far as to invite me and Fred down for breakfast to show there were no hard feelings.

Fred was wide awake now. He must have been eavesdropping and heard about the sausage.

"What do you say, Fred?" I asked. "Want to get some breakfast at Aunt Bonnie's?" He barked twice and ran to the door.

"I must have really pissed him off this time," I said after listening to Bonnie tell me about Chuck's latest effort to make my life miserable. "Either that or he's afraid I'm getting too close to the truth."

Bonnie put her unfinished breakfast down for Fred and refilled my coffee before I could wave her off. "Negligent homicide is a felony, Jake. Aren't you worried? Maybe you can get a lawyer before the sheriff comes to get you."

I didn't tell her I already knew about the DA. Julie had asked me to keep it quiet, so I tried to play it down. "Not really, Bon. I can't imagine the DA trying to pin Lonnie's death on me. I think Chuck is trying to get me to back off. Maybe he thinks I'll run away and leave him alone. Whatever his reason, it really doesn't concern me anymore. I've got a lot more important things to think about now that I've asked Julie to marry me."

Bonnie nearly slammed the coffee pot on the table and reached out to hug me. "Oh, Jake. I'm so happy for you. She reminds me so much of my Diane." She let me out of her bear hug and sat back in her chair, and said in a less cheerful voice, "I know you would have fallen for her. She was so beautiful, but at last she can rest in peace."

Bonnie caught me off guard with her last remark. "At last she can rest in peace? What's that supposed to mean?"

"Did I say that? Silly me. I don't know what I was thinking," she answered while subconsciously wiping a few drops of the coffee that had splashed on the table. "But seriously, Jake, Chuck has some powerful friends. I don't think you should take this so lightly."

I was completely out of breath when I reached my cabin door. Bonnie lived the proverbial stone's throw from me, but it was all uphill in the thin air of eight thousand feet and I ran the last ten or twenty yards when I heard my phone ringing. I had left it in my cabin in my haste to get a free breakfast earlier. Of course, the phone stopped ringing when I answered it, but there was a message. It was from my old boss. He wanted to talk to me about a job.

Fred was over by the motor home when I finally got off the phone and went outside to see what he was up to. He was sniffing and scratching at the cargo door that gave access to the area under the couch. It was a couch that made into a bed with storage underneath it. He ran over to me when he saw me, barked and then ran back to the motor home.

"What's in there that's got you so upset, Fred?" I asked and bent down to open the door.

Chatter flew out of the compartment and headed for the nearest tree, with Fred one step behind. Poor Fred wasn't fast enough and the squirrel made it to safety only to start teasing Fred with his chatter. I laughed, then went back to the storage compartment to see how the squirrel got in there in the first place.

There were pine nuts, chewed-up foam rubber and paper everywhere. He had made himself at home. On second thought, maybe Chatter wasn't a 'he' at all. She had made a nest with the paper. How she got in was a mystery. The storage compartment had been closed and locked. Then I saw where she had chewed a hole in the bottom of my couch. She must have come through the door damaged by Julie's crew and chewed her way into the compartment.

I recognized the paper she had made her nest with as Ray's manuscript. It had to be the missing pages that my scanner ate the night I copied it. When I took a closer look I found it barely readable. What my scanner had failed to destroy, Chatter finished.

Putting the pieces of the manuscript pages back together on my kitchen was like trying to assemble a jigsaw puzzle without all the pieces. I finished just as Julie came in the door.

She put some groceries on the kitchen counter, and then came over to give me a kiss. "So this is how you spend your time when I'm not around. Let me guess. You found a new technique to overcome writer's block."

I kissed her back; not the kind of kiss one gives a new lover. It was more of a married twenty-year kiss a husband gives when he's keeping a secret from his wife. I didn't want to tell her about the loan from my sister or the job offer until I had those birds in my hand. I had visions of getting on my knees with a ring I was going to buy with whatever money was left over from the loan once I caught up on my bills. I knew it wouldn't be enough to actually buy the ring, but maybe my credit was still good enough to use the money as a down payment.

"Not a bad idea, smarty pants. Maybe I should copyright it and call it Julie's guide to finding your muse," I said.

She smiled and tried to read the puzzle. I got up from my chair and stood beside her trying to get a better view. I nearly jumped when she put her arm around my waist.

"Does that say what I think it says?" she asked without taking her eyes off the scraps of paper that read, *"The hipacrit johnson even fathered a child out of wed lock she was a pretty little thing they named Shelia and thats why we never wnet to church again."*

"If you think it says the good reverend is Shelia's father," I answered.

"Julie squeezed my waist, then let me go and went back to the groceries. "Hope you don't mind eating off of paper plates. I'm not into washing dishes without a dishwasher."

I quit trying to decipher the rest of Ray's masterpiece and went over to help her prepare our dinner. "You were right about the DA," I said while opening a bottle of white wine I found in one of the bags. To my amazement, it was still cold. "Bonnie called to tell me Chuck's trying to get the warrant you told me about. He just won't quit."

Julie produced some plastic wine glasses from another bag and placed two of them on the counter. They were the kind with long stems and resembled the crystal I had borrowed from Bonnie. "Are you sure it's Chuck?" Julie asked.

"Who else could it be?" I asked while filling the glasses.

"Well, there's Jonathan and Shelia to start with, and what about that guy you put away for life back in Missouri? Didn't you say he was well connected?"

Julie had to remind me of Hal. He had murdered my brother-in-law last year and wasn't even a suspect until I stuck my nose in to free my sister.

"I doubt if it was Hal." I answered after setting my wine down on the table and going to the door. Fred decided to join us and was scratching at the door to be let in. He must have smelled the chicken. He ignored me and went straight to Julie.

"No, it has to be Chuck. Bonnie got the info from Margot. She thinks I should get out of Dodge until it all cools over," I answered. I tried to make a joke out of the situation, but realized I sounded serious when I didn't see her smile.

Julie came away from the kitchen counter with two plates piled with rotisserie chicken and potato salad. She placed the larger portion in front of me then bent down to kiss me on the cheek. "Tell you what, Chicken Little, I'll make a call and see if the DA got his warrant yet."

I started to say something, but she was already on her cell phone. I waited and listened the best I could. She was asking a friend at work to check the computer for any wants or warrants on me. I had forgotten that wildlife agents had the same access to computer files as the state police. She was telling her friend that it would look better if she didn't run the check herself. The whole process didn't take more than a few minutes.

"Looks like you're clean, Jake," she said after hanging up and pinching me on my spare tire. "There are a dozen

Martins with outstanding warrants, but none by the name of Jacob. I never realized what a common name I'll be taking."

She smiled and added, "You know you really should get more exercise, Chubby."

I didn't know whether to kiss her or pout. We weren't even married yet and already she was acting like a wife. I chose the former and got up, held her head in my hands and kissed her like never before. Evidently it was too long a kiss. Fred broke it up by barking at us.

I tried to act annoyed. "What do you want, you mangy mutt? Don't tell me you're jealous?"

He wasn't buying my act and barked again before running over to the kitchen counter. Julie had to laugh and broke away from my embrace.

"Michelle said she'd call if any warrants show up," she said while walking over to Fred.

"Looks like you won't have to leave me all alone in the dark by myself tonight," she added with a wink.

The nice thing about a Golden Retriever is you don't need a garbage disposal. Except for the bones, the uneaten chicken didn't go to waste. That one wink was all it took to carry Julie off to bed. Of course, knowing that I wouldn't be arrested anytime soon, helped too.

Another thing about Goldens is that they are always hungry. Fred had no trouble scarfing down the leftover scrambled eggs and sausage we had at Bonnie's the next morning. I still didn't trust my phone and the NSA so

Fred and I walked down the hill to tell her about my reprieve from the clutches of the sheriff. She must be psychic, for breakfast was waiting for us.

"How'd you know we were coming, Bonnie?" I asked when I saw the table all laid out with a huge plate of eggs, my favorite sausage links, orange juice and toast.

She gave me her Cheshire grin and said, "When you didn't leave yesterday after Julie came home early, and you didn't follow her when she left this morning, I figured she must have fixed it for you somehow. After all, she is a cop of sorts."

Surely I was becoming paranoid; I started to wonder if Bonnie had my cabin bugged. Either that or Fred was blabbing all my secrets in exchange for food.

"Please don't tell anyone," I said. "She could get in a lot of trouble. She ran a computer check for wants and warrants. Seems the DA didn't get his warrant; at least not yet. But if I don't find a way to shut Chuck down soon, I'll be on the next plane to Mexico."

Bonnie's grin faded. "Wait here, Jake. I have something for you that I should have given you long ago." She was up and headed for her junk room before I could ask what it was. It was actually her second bedroom, but I peeked in one day on my way to the bathroom. It was filled from wall to wall and floor to ceiling with what most people considered junk: boxes of garage-sale finds, broken pottery, pictures, books, stacks of old newspapers… well just think of the word hoarder and you know what I mean.

I helped myself to another cup of coffee while waiting for her to return. Fred followed me to the kitchen; I assume hoping for another handout. I was nearly finished with the coffee and ready to check on her, in case one of the boxes had fallen on her, when she reappeared holding some old newspaper clippings. She handed me a page of wedding announcements.

"Okay, Bon Bon, I'll bite. What am I looking for?" I asked when a quick scan didn't mention Charlie Randolph.

Bonnie looked at me like I'd just flunked a final, and then pretended to hit herself upside the head. "Silly me. Here, read this one first," she said, handing me a yellowed paper. This time the announcement I was meant to see had been circled in faded-red ink.

"Mr. and Mrs. Montgomery are proud to announce the engagement of their daughter to Charlie Randolph," I read aloud. I didn't have to finish. It would have taken too long for this announcement took up half the page. The name, Montgomery, looked familiar, so I reread the first clipping. Imbedded in all the verbose announcements was a short, one-liner announcing the wedding of Hazel Montgomery to Howard Carson.

"So she dumped Chuck in favor of this guy, Howard?" I paused to check the dates. "Looks like three months later. What does this have to do with anything?"

Bonnie smiled and went on, "Shelia's maiden name is Carson."

"Are you saying Chuck is Shelia's father? That can't be."

Bonnie gave me her confused look. "Why do you say that?"

"Sit down, Bon. I've been keeping something from you that you should hear." I was afraid she was going to drop the shoebox, so I reached out for it and set it down on the table.

"Fred found the missing pages of your father's manuscript."

"Fred?" she asked, raising her brows.

"Well, he didn't actually find them, but he led me to them. Chatter had got into my motor home and took them from the scanner to make a nest, but that's not important. What is important is that your father claims Reverend Johnson is Shelia's father."

"No shit? All this time he's been giving her money and watching her back. Maybe daddy got it wrong. Those clippings kind of say Chuck is her father. Don't they?" she asked, pointing to the shoebox.

"I suppose. Maybe he was wrong about Jonathan too."

"Too?" she answered. "You know about Jonathan?"

"Yeah, I read enough of your father's manuscript to know about Chuck and Margot, and Margot's husband having a vasectomy during his first marriage. Old Chuck must have been one heck of a stud in his day?"

Bonnie smiled and took another drink before continuing. She had a far-away look in her eyes. "And a lot better looking. I had a crush on him myself, but at least now you know why Charlie hates you so much. He thinks he's protecting his daughter."

"Does Jonathan know?" I asked.

"No. Margot sent Jonathan to live with his father after they divorced. Nobody ever told him he wasn't his real father."

"In Minnesota?" I asked.

"How'd you know that?"

"A little birdie told me," I answered, using her phrase, from the day before, in an attempt to lighten the mood.

It seemed to work. I did make her smile, so I told the truth. "His accent, Bon. The only people I know of, who talk like that, are from the frozen north." I didn't know what more to say. Fortunately, I didn't have to; my cell phone started to ring and when I looked at the caller ID I saw it was my sister's husband.

"Hey Bon, it's Julie," I lied. I didn't want her to overhear any juicy details about my loan. "Hope you don't mind if I call her back from my place."

Fred and I returned to my cabin with the news clippings Bonnie had given me. He didn't want to leave as long as there was still food on her counter, but I

promised him a big treat when we got home. This time I
didn't try to run up the hill. Maybe Julie was right. I
either needed more exercise or had to go on a diet. The
mountain air was making me winded.

Fred soon forgot about the treat I had promised him
when he spotted Chatter calling him from a nearby blue
spruce. I let him try to catch the squirrel and went into
the cabin to return Ira's call. My cell phone rang before I
could start the call. "Hi, Bonnie. What'd I forget?" I
asked while checking for my wallet and keys. I had a bad
habit of misplacing both of them.

"Jake, there's a county truck coming up your way.
You better get Fred in the house. It's the dog catcher."

"Thanks, Bonnie. You're a sweetheart," I said and
hung up my phone. The county did have leash laws
which most people up here in the hills ignored, and the
county rarely enforced. Still, I thought it would be wise to
fetch Fred just in case.

Fred was sitting at the base of the big blue spruce
waiting for Chatter to get closer. I thanked my lucky stars
for that squirrel keeping Fred close and called for him.
When that didn't work, I rushed back to the kitchen to
get some kind of treat that might get him away from
Chatter. Julie's cookies were still sitting on the table, so I
grabbed them and ran back outside. Luckily, Fred liked
cookies better than squirrel-in-a-tree and I was able to
bribe him away from Chatter. It wasn't a minute too

soon. The animal control officer was out of her truck and headed my way.

"Stay and be quiet," I said to Fred then threw him another cookie and went back outside to greet my new visitor. Of course Fred had the last word and started barking to go out with me.

"Morning, Officer," I said as she placed one foot on the first step of my porch stairs then stopped to look up at me.

"Hi, Jacob," she said.

Do I know her? I asked myself before answering her. "You can call me Jake. Unless you're here to arrest me for running loose without a leash, then Mister Martin will do."

A small smile formed at the corners of her mouth. I couldn't help notice the lack of lipstick or any other makeup. It gave her a tomboy look which I found very attractive.

"You don't remember me, do you?" she asked, holding out her hand. "We went to high school together. I'm Sherry Franklin."

"Sorry I didn't recognize you, Sherry," I answered while shifting Julie's bag of cookies to my left hand and reaching out to take Sherry's hand. "What brings you up this way? It's not often we get a visit from animal control. Come to think of it. We never get a visit from you guys."

"Hope those aren't peanut butter cookies you were eating?" she asked, quickly withdrawing her hand. "You probably don't remember when I almost died from them."

I subconsciously wiped my hand on my pants. "You're that Sherry?" I asked. "My God, I'd almost forgotten about that." The cafeteria never served peanut products after that.

She watched me wipe my hands as though I had the plague. "It's okay. I carry a couple epipens in the truck, just in case."

"An epipen?" I asked.

She finally smiled. "It's like a syringe, only smaller. If I ever come in contact with peanuts, I can give myself an injection of epinephrine."

"Oh," I replied. I didn't feel like telling her I already knew what the epipen was and that my question had been rhetorical.

"That was a long time ago," she said. "I had a crush on you when we went to Lakewood High. You and were in my second period English class."

She stepped back, removing her foot from the porch step. Her smile faded and she reached into her back pocket. "I was supposed to pick up your dog for running loose and give you this summons to appear in court," she said, holding the summons but not quite giving it to me. "But I can see, or should I say hear, that he's in the house and not running loose so I'll just give you the summons."

Call it a premonition or a sixth sense, but whatever you call it, I could feel she wasn't happy serving me. She looked so vulnerable. Like a child having to read aloud in front of the class. I was beginning to feel sorry for her.

"Where did you get the idea I let my dog run loose?"

"I can't say, Jake, other than someone filed a complaint," she answered without looking at me. Then she completely changed the subject while staring at the ground. "It's okay, Jake. I know you don't remember me. I was not much to look at in those days; just a fat teenage girl with a crush on the cutest guy in class."

I started to mumble something. Sherry didn't wait. "Tell you what, Jake," she said, sticking the summons in her back pocket. "I'll say I wasn't able to deliver it."

She quit studying the ground and looked up at me. I think I saw a tear. "Did you eat any of those?" she asked.

"No. I used them to bribe my dog to stay put."

Then out of the blue she reached up and pulled me toward her and kissed me.

"Thanks, Jake. I've been dreaming about that ever since I saw your name on the summons," she said, heading back to her truck. "Watch your back. Someone is out to get you."

I stood there watching her go. A couple weeks ago, I would have asked her to stay, but now I felt guilty about the kiss and thoughts of what it could have led to. Then out of nowhere it hit me. I knew who killed Lonnie.

"Sherry," I called out before she got into her truck."

She turned at the mention of her name.

"Sherry," I repeated. "Can I see one of those pens?"

I'd expected bewilderment, but she was smiling. "Was the kiss that bad?" she asked.

"No. It was great," I answered while walking over to her truck. "I only asked because you just gave me a great idea on how to finish a short story I'm working on. It would make a fantastic murder weapon. I don't need the pen itself, just the case it comes in so I can describe it correctly."

She opened her truck door and rummaged through the center console, then handed me a case. "Take this one, Jake. It's left over from the last time I had to inject myself."

Fred was waiting at the door when I returned to the cabin. He ran past me, straight for the tree and Chatter before I had a chance to grab him. "Oh well," I said aloud while pushing the recall button on my cell phone. "Go ahead and run loose, Freddie. Something tells me she won't be back anytime soon."

Chatter seemed to know Fred's limits. She would get just close enough so when he jumped he could almost bite her. I finally took a seat on my rocker so I could watch the circus when Ira picked up his phone.

"What did you ever do to the guy, Jake? Lucky he's not connected to the mafia or I'm sure there'd be a contract on you," Ira asked after he told me my loan had been wired to my bank already and I brought him up to date on my dilemma with Chuck and the DA.

"He thinks I killed his illegitimate daughter's husband."

"His what?"

"It's a long story, Ira," I answered. I had moved out of my rocker to watch the road just to be sure Sherry didn't change her mind.

"The short version is that I was in charge of a barbeque grill earlier this month that blew up killing a neighbor. It turns out the guy was Charlie Randolph's son-in-law. Charlie's been trying to crucify me ever since. First with a wrongful death suit, then he comes up with this BS felony charge; and to top it off, I got a visit from animal control this morning over Fred running loose. I can't imagine what he'll do next."

"Well, I can tell you what he won't do. He won't be getting the DA to prosecute anytime soon. He doesn't have enough evidence, but watch your back, Jake. Randolph knows some very powerful people."

That was the second time in less than an hour someone told me to watch my back. I wanted to tell Ira that it wouldn't be necessary much longer since I now knew who killed Lonnie. I immediately called Bonnie after Ira hung up.

"Hi, Jake, is Fred okay?"

I pictured Bonnie's innocent smile and hated myself for what I had to do. "Yeah, unless he manages to catch Chatter. The dog catcher just warned me to keep Fred on a leash. Hey, Bon, can I ask a favor?"

"Of course, Jake, I don't have much, but whatever it is, it's yours."

"You're the best, Bon Bon, but I didn't call for a loan," I stammered, trying to think how to tell her what I wanted. "Does Margot still have her Saturday dinner parties?"

"You want her to invite you?" she asked.

"I was hoping Julie and I could come as your guest without telling anyone beforehand. I'm afraid certain people wouldn't come if they knew I was coming."

She hesitated before answering. I wish I could see her expression over the phone. It must be one of pure confusion. "Well, it's not my party, but I'm sure Margot won't mind if you guys tag along. What's it all about anyway?" she asked in a very suspicious voice.

"I have something for Chuck that should get him to stop his harassment. I'm afraid he won't show if he knows I'm coming."

The pause on her end of the line was a little too long before she answered. "You're not going to tell him I told you about Lonnie, I hope?"

"No, Bon, it's nothing like that. I won't say anything you told me."

"Thank you, Jake." Then another pause before she spoke again. "Can you tell me what it is?"

I had to think fast and make up something believable. "I know you don't care for him much more than I do, so you can't tell anyone, not even Margot. My brother-in-law, the lawyer, says I have grounds for a huge libel and harassment suit. I'm going to tell Chuck to back off or get Ira to sue him."

"Ooo, I don't want to miss that. Why don't you guys pick me up at five on Saturday and we can all go down to Margot's together?"

"You got it, Bon, and thanks," I said then disconnected. I couldn't see her expression and was just as happy that she couldn't see the joy on my face. My plan to trap Lonnie's killer, or what was becoming a plan, was beginning to take shape, but first I had to take care of business and call my old boss back before Julie got home.

"You sure you want me to do this?" Julie asked, holding scissors in one hand and a clump of my hair in the other. "It's not too late to change your mind. I'm sure a barber can repair it."

"Keep cutting, M'love, or are you afraid all the girls will find me sexy now that bald is in?" Julie went back to snipping off my hair without any more objections. A minute later we were beyond the point of no return.

She had come home wearing a blond wig to cover her own baldness. She had seen her doctor and made the appointment for radiation treatment earlier in the day, then went and had all her beautiful hair cut off before it fell out on its own. I had insisted she cut my hair, but she had refused until I had taken matters in my own hand and nicked my scalp. I agreed not to do the same to Fred.

"I wish you wouldn't take the job, Jake," she said as I watched my dirty-blond hair hit the floor. "My disability pay is more than enough to get by until I go back to work, and I will really need you here to tell me how gorgeous I look bald."

I had agreed to meet with my old boss in the morning to discuss going back to work. The company's effort to trim expenses by firing me and several hundred others two years ago had backfired. The bean-counters thought they could save mega bucks by outsourcing our work offshore. The math worked for them as they would no longer be paying half our pay out in benefits, but the team in Bangalore failed to live up to expectations. There were so many bugs and security holes in the new software that management finally had to scrap it and go back to the old code. Now they need some of us back to maintain it.

"Tell you what, Gorgeous. I'll tell him I need to work from home. He can take it or leave it."

"Thank you, Jake. It was beginning to look like a rewrite of The Gift of the Magi. Only I donated my hair instead of selling it and you didn't buy the rings yet, did you?"

I could feel wet drops on my exposed scalp. I wanted to wipe them off, but the scissors were cutting hair around my ears and didn't think this was a good time to make any sudden movements. "Not yet. Would you like to go pick them out next Saturday on the way back from Margot's?"

"Margot's? What are you talking about, Goofy?"

"Oh, I forgot to tell you. I solved Lonnie's murder today and invited us to Margot's weekly dinner party. All the interested parties will be there so it will be the perfect time to set my trap."

We spent the rest of the afternoon discussing my plan over pizza and beer at a local restaurant in downtown Evergreen. She thought it would be a good place to try out my new haircut, but wasn't ready to go without her own wig. I didn't manage to turn a single head. It was amazing how many men shaved their heads.

Julie managed to politely point out a few flaws in my plan and made suggestions to make it work. She also made me promise to delete the ad selling my motor home. She had big plans on visiting the major national parks, starting with the Grand Canyon, once the chemo was over. Her grandfather had taken her on a trip there when she was only ten. It was what made her choose a career that involved animals and working outdoors.

Chapter 16

Julie and Bonnie did most of the talking on our trip to Margot's home in Cherry Creek. Julie suggested taking her car rather than my beat-up Jeep or her state-owned SUV. She had joked about the neighbors calling the police if we drove up to Margot's in my Wagoneer.

They were still chatting away when we made our grand entrance, but stopped when Margot met us at the door. "You're late, Bonnie. We finished dinner twenty minutes ago."

Bonnie didn't act surprised. "At least we brought dessert. Can we come in?"

Margot didn't answer and led us to her great room. Everyone stopped talking the minute I walked into the room.

Chuck was sitting alone in a huge, overstuffed, leather recliner. Shelia, Carlos and Reverend Johnson were facing him from the matching sofa.

"I'd like to introduce Jake's new fiancé to everyone," Bonnie said before they could recover. "This is Julie Bartowski, she's a game warden."

Chuck looked over at Margot then spoke before Bonnie could finish. "What the hell is he doing here?"

Margot kept her cool and rose to greet Julie, ignoring Chuck's remark. "I'm so happy for you, Dear," she said, giving her a little peck on the cheek.

Julie had brought a batch of her homemade cookies and handed them off to me so she could return Margot's greeting.

"Let me put those on a plate," Bonnie said, taking the cookies from me.

The reverend got up and came over to Julie the second Margot stepped back. "A game warden? Now there's an interesting occupation," he said, extending a hand. "I'm Reverend Johnson."

"I sort of fell into it after college," Julie said, returning the handshake. "I wanted to be a park ranger so I studied zoology. After taking the state test, I got a call from the DOW."

"That's a crock," Chuck said from the safety of his recliner. "Whoever heard it called Zoe-ol-ogy. She's as much a game warden as me. She can't even pronounce zoo-ol-ogy?"

Julie couldn't help but smile and reached into her purse. "I've got my badge in here somewhere," she said and made a show of dropping a few things on the floor. We didn't know how to make it seem natural when we cooked up our plan the day before. Chuck made it so easy for us.

"Is that an epipen?" Shelia asked when she saw Julie pick up the injector I had borrowed from Sherry the dog catcher.

"So that's what it is," Julie answered. "Jake's dog found it and Jake gave it to me thinking a poacher might have dropped it. My purse can be a bottomless pit sometimes. I'd completely forgotten about it."

"What the hell is a hippy pen?" Chuck asked.

"Epipen, Chuck. It's for people with severe allergies," Shelia answered. "You inject yourself with ephedrine when you get stung by a bee or eat peanuts. Carlos is always losing his. I wonder if it's his?"

Margot seemed to be getting impatient and broke in, "Maybe Jake can tell us more when he tells you why he's here. Bonnie says he has something to tell us."

Bonnie stopped dead and turned around to look at me with guilty eyes. She hadn't gone two feet toward the kitchen. "I'm sorry, Jake. She is my sister," she said while giving Margot a nasty look; it was the kind of look sister's share when they're not happy with one another for telling secrets.

"Just get this bullshit over with, will you. Saturday's are my busiest day. I should be at the dealership instead of listening to whatever pathetic plea you have." Chuck said, staring me in the eyes. A cold stare would be an understatement. His eyes were so dark I couldn't see what color they were. Bonnie started to protest, but Margot nudged her with a foot to stop her, so she left for the kitchen without a word.

Chuck didn't seem to notice. He didn't wait for me or anyone else to answer. "And if you think you can get me to back off with some stupid plea for mercy, you've got another think coming."

Reverend Johnson didn't give me a chance to answer Chuck. "I must say, I'm a little put out too, Jake. Shelia and I really have much better things to do today. We only stayed because Margot insisted, so please say what you need to so I can get back to preparing tomorrow's sermon."

"Well put, Reverend," Chuck said. He was trying to get up, but the cushions were too soft for his mass. He finally sat back down when no one offered to help him.

He looked over at me with contempt and said, "So say what you came for so we can all go."

Bonnie came back with the cookies before I could answer Chuck. She gave Chuck a not-too friendly look and put the cookies on the coffee table without a comment.

Julie saw her chance and picked up the plate, offering Carlos the first one. "I made these myself, Carlos. I hope you like chocolate."

The boy seemed to hesitate, looking at the reverend for approval. Johnson nodded okay and the cookie was gone in a second. "Can I have another?" he asked the pastor.

Once again, Reverend Johnson nodded, but added, "One more. You need to save some for the other guests."

Julie set the plate on the table for the others to help themselves. Chuck turned up his nose at them when Shelia offered him one before taking one for herself.

"Well," Chuck said. "If everyone is done stuffing their faces, I'd like to hear Mister Martin's earth shattering announcement."

"These are really good," Shelia said as though Chuck wasn't in the room. "What is your recipe, Julie?"

"It's an old family secret. We use a full cup of peanut butter in every batch."

Reverend Johnson spit out his coffee and grabbed a half eaten cookie from Carlos. "You said they were chocolate!" he yelled. "Why didn't you tell me they had peanut butter?"

Shelia looked like a vampire just drained her blood. "Give me that pen. Quick!" she yelled.

Julie handed her the epipen. This time she didn't have to fumble. Our plan called for an instant reaction.

Johnson grabbed the pen from Shelia before she could inject Carlos. "Don't use that one. You'll kill him."

Everyone became so quiet; you could hear a woodpecker outside pounding a tree for his dinner.

The scene was playing out better than I could have possibly hoped, but it was time to break the news. "Don't worry, Reverend. Carlos will be fine. There's no peanut butter in the cookies, and that isn't your injector. The police have that one," I said. "They're checking for prints and analyzing the contents as we speak." The last part was pure fiction. I needed to convince the reverend we were on to him.

Reverend Johnson put his elbows on his legs and his face in his hands. "I'm not sorry. He was an evil man who wouldn't leave us alone. When Shelia moved in with me and he couldn't beat her anymore, he threatened to tell the congregation about my past. He would have ruined everything."

"Shut up, Daddy!" Shelia yelled at the reverend. "He can't prove any of this."

"You're forgetting about the injector, Shelia," I said. "I'm sure they will find the reverend's prints on it and the fact it wasn't filled with ephedrine."

Johnson raised his head and looked up at Shelia. "It's okay, Baby. I couldn't live with the guilt much longer. I'm glad Jake figured it out." Then he turned to me. "How did you know, Jake?"

Julie slipped into the kitchen to call for backup when all eyes were on me to answer. "The epipen; you can thank Charlie for that. He's been trying to crucify me ever since the accident. He's harassed me with lawsuits, criminal charges and even dog catchers. The dog catcher was his downfall. She carried an epipen just like yours. I knew Lonnie couldn't have died from first and second degree burns, but didn't realize he was poisoned until I saw her injector and then I remembered you had one just like it. I already knew about Shelia being your daughter. You're not the first father who killed to protect his children."

I paused long enough for everyone else to grasp what I had said, then continued, "What did you use anyway, Reverend?"

Johnson actually smiled. "Aconitine, I extracted from wolfsbane. The mountain meadows are covered with it."

Shelia stared at me then started to cry. "The bastard wouldn't leave us alone," she said between sobs. "Beating me wasn't enough. He said he'd tell I was driving the Corvette if I didn't move back in with him."

Bonnie looked like she'd seen a ghost. "Lonnie wasn't driving?"

"No. He was too drunk and made me drive. I didn't even have my license yet. I'm so sorry, Bonnie."

"Oh my God," Bonnie said and sat down. "I killed the wrong person."

Once more we could all hear the woodpecker. His pecking didn't last nearly as long this time before I cut in. "No, Bon Bon. It was the reverend. Peanut oil is nearly harmless unless it's ingested. The oil you put in the Bactine couldn't be absorbed in sufficient quantities to kill even the most allergic."

She looked at me in horror. "You knew about the Bactine?"

I simply nodded my head. I had planned on telling her when we were alone. Now everyone knew she tried to kill Lonnie.

Chuck spoke before I could continue. "Reverend Johnson is your father?" he asked Shelia. "You said I was

your father! You even showed me the birth certificate!"
For the first time since I met him, I was thankful Chuck
had bad manners. Not that anyone would soon forget
Bonnie's confession.

"I'm sorry, Charlie," Shelia answered. "It was
Lonnie's idea. He made the phony birth certificate when
he found out about you and my mother's engagement."
she answered and started crying again.

"Was that before or after he tried blackmailing me?"
Chuck asked.

"Lonnie was blackmailing you?" Margot asked. Her
eyes had become as dark as Chuck's. "What on earth
for?"

Chuck answered like she was one of his employees
who had just scratched the paint on a showroom car.
"That's none of your damn business, but before Jake
goes running off his mouth, it had nothing to do with
any of this. Lonnie was always looking for a way to make
a buck without working for it. He got what he deserved."

"It was probably the fragging, Margot," I said. Chuck
was right, it had nothing to do with Lonnie's murder, but
I couldn't help myself.

"And if my guess is right, Johnson is also Carlos'
grandfather," I said to Chuck before turning toward
Johnson.

"I'm sorry, Reverend. Julie had you checked out after
I read about you in Ray's book. You aren't his foster

parent. The county would never give a child to an ex-con."

Julie turned away from the conversation and went to the front door. No one seemed surprised when she let in two uniformed cops and a detective.

In contrast to the trip down a few hours earlier, the girls hardly spoke on the way back up the mountain. When Julie wasn't dozing off, her mind seemed to be elsewhere. The doctors had warned us this might happen, so I let her rest while trying to keep my answers to Bonnie's questions short.

"How did you know about the Corvette, Jake?" Bonnie asked.

"I did some digging after you gave me those clippings on the hit and run. I found one of the witnesses and she told me it was a Daytona Blue Corvette that ran over Diane. I did some more snooping and found Jonathan's vette had been repainted and its original color was, you guessed it, Daytona Blue." I stopped talking long enough to check on Julie.

"Jonathan came clean and told me the car was owned by Lonnie's uncle up in Fort Collins, and that he borrowed it the night of Diane's hit and run," I said once I saw Julie was sound asleep. "When his uncle died last year, Lonnie got the car and promptly sold it to Jonathan."

"Do you think anyone will press charges against me?" Bonnie asked. Her gaze was fixed on the passing scenery. It was like she was asking someone outside the car.

"I doubt it, Bon. What proof would the DA have if he did decide to go after you? Just make sure you get rid of that Bactine bottle when you get home."

"I already did, Jake. I already did."

I should have been feeling great. I just solved a murder case and a twenty year old manslaughter case and was about to break up a poaching ring, but the two women who meant the most to me were far from cheerful.

I let Bonnie off at her place and then drove up to my cabin with Julie. Jonathan was waiting for us on my porch. Luckily, Julie's nap had given her the energy she needed to finish my nightmares.

"Hello, Jonathan. Have you met Officer Bartowski?" I said after we joined him.

"You sure I'll remain anonymous?" he said to Julie.

"Scouts honor," she said without raising her hand, or offering it for a handshake.

"Come on in, Jon. Let's go on the back deck and have a warm beer," I said while opening my front door.

Fred didn't give me his usual greeting. He didn't even go outside. I guess he wasn't about to leave me unprotected. Jonathan and I went out to the back deck with Fred while Julie followed.

I took three beers from my beer cooler. I opened one for Julie and passed it on to Jonathan when she waved it off, then opened one for myself.

"How'd you know it was Chuck?" Jon asked after taking a long drink.

I followed his lead and took a drink too before answering. "To be honest, after Alec confessed, I thought the case was closed, but the fact that Mario was working for him when Mario had about the same salesman skills as an offshore telemarketer got me to thinking there was more to it. My dog speaks better English.

"I knew whoever planted the bow was a roofer for he left a huge smear of tar on my motor home when he put your bow under my bed. At first I thought it was you, but you never get your hands dirty. Chuck put Mario up to the poaching as a way to finance the meth operation. When the law was getting too close, he had Mario plant your bow to frame me, and then left a tip on the hotline on where to find it."

"No way is that hypocrite my father or I wouldn't be doing this. Real fathers don't ignore their children for thirty-five years and only try to make amends when they think the end is near," Jonathan said while taking a folded piece of paper from his pocket and sliding it across the table. "Here's my statement. In writing and signed like you asked."

Then he turned to Julie. "When will I get that reward, Miss Barkowsky?"

"Bartowski, with a tee," she answered.

The last time I'd seen her so business like, she had me in handcuffs.

"Sorry," Jon said. "Did you bring it with you?"

She surprised me and slid Jonathan a piece of paper. "This is your code. You'll need it to collect the reward if we get a conviction."

Jonathan smiled at her wickedly. "Oh, you'll get the conviction okay, and I hope you take down that pompous ass."

Epilogue

I had to find a place away from the crowd where I could let Fred out so I chose an overlook far from the Grand Canyon's visitor center.

It had been nearly a year before Jonathan got his reward. Unfortunately, Charlie Randolph didn't. Mario confessed to the poaching and being Alex's meth partner, but there was no hard evidence to prove Chuck had bankrolled the operation and his lawyers got him off without so much as a reprimand. Mario relied on the public defender and got twenty years in Sterling.

Julie would have received a commendation for her work if she had lived. Her cancer made a ferocious comeback soon after we married. Except for potty breaks, Fred never left her side the entire time. I know, because I didn't either.

Fred seemed to know it was Julie's ashes we were spreading in the soft breeze. He actually had tears in his eyes.

ABOUT THE AUTHOR

Richard is working on his third career. His first was as a carpenter and roofer for twenty years while working his way through college. With a BS in Math he spent the next twenty-five years as a successful software engineer by working on the Space Shuttle at both Vandenberg AFB, and Johnson Space Center. He then went on to start Master Mind SofTools where he developed software for fortune 500 companies. After taking early retirement in 2007, he moved to Warsaw, Missouri and built a home on the water with a view to die for. Richard is currently working on the third novel in his To Die For series.

Made in the USA
Middletown, DE
17 July 2018